W9-BPJ-451

# The Last
# White Knight

# The Last White Knight

## Tami Hoag

**THORNDIKE**
CHIVERS

This Large Print edition is published by Thorndike Press®, Waterville, Maine USA and by BBC Audiobooks, Ltd, Bath, England.

Published in 2006 in the U.S. by arrangement with The Bantam Dell Publishing Group, a division of Random House, Inc.

Published in 2006 in the U.K. by arrangement with The Bantam Dell Publishing Group, a division of Random House, Inc.

| U.S. Hardcover | 0-7862-8867-1 (Americana) |
| U.K. Hardcover | 10: 1 4056 3882 6 (Chivers Large Print) |
| U.K. Hardcover | 13: 978 1 405 63882 1 |
| U.K Softcover | 10: 1 4056 3883 4 (Camden Large Print) |
| U.K. Softcover | 13: 978 1 405 63883 8 |

The text of this Large Print edition is unabridged. Other aspects of the book may vary from the original edition.

Set in 16 pt. Plantin by Myrna S. Raven

Printed in the United States on permanent paper.

**British Library Cataloguing-in-Publication Data available**

**Library of Congress Cataloging-in-Publication Data**

Hoag, Tami.
    The last white knight / by Tami Hoag.
        p. cm. — (Thorndike Press large print Americana series)
    ISBN 0-7862-8867-1 (lg. print : hc : alk. paper)
    1. Group homes for youth — Fiction.   2. Large type books.   I. Title.
PS3558.O333L37 2006b
    813'.54—dc22                                                    2006019509

# The Last White Knight

# — 1 —

"What we need is a white knight." Lillian Johnson looked up toward the big house, worry creasing her forehead above the rims of her glasses. She stood stiffly at the nose of her Volvo, slender shoulders set as if to take a blow, the summer evening breeze just teasing the ends of silver hair cut in a sleek pageboy. In her blouse with the Peter Pan collar and pleated skirt, she looked like a librarian about to be set upon by a mob of book-burning fanatics.

The sidewalk in front of the house was crowded with unhappy people, neighbors who were not inclined to feel neighborly toward the new folks on the block. Many were holding hand-lettered signs aloft. *No Delinquents! Runaways Go Home! Citizens for Family Neighborhoods.* A news crew from the local television station was capturing the action on videotape.

Lynn Shaw frowned as a breeze caught at strands of her long black hair and whipped them across her face. She raked them back with one hand, green eyes fixed on the crowd. "There's no such thing as white knights." She leaned down into the trunk of her middle-aged Buick and emerged with a box of kitchen utensils cradled in her arms. "Besides, I'll be damned if I'm waiting around for some man to come and save me."

Leaving her friend and employer behind, she stepped up onto the boulevard and started toward the house with a determined stride. She was a counselor, after all. She knew how to handle people. She had the skills to defuse the situation — provided she didn't lose her temper. Of course, there was an ever-present danger of her losing her temper these days.

The relocation of Horizon House should have been simple. Call a moving van, pack a few boxes, change the letterhead on the stationery. The home had been in its former location for three years without incident. Lynn doubted if most of the citizens of Rochester, Minnesota, had had any idea it existed until the building that housed Horizon's residents had been scheduled for demolition to make room for a new hotel. And the Horizon staff might have pulled off the move to this nondescript house with the neighbors going on in self-absorbed, quiet bliss if it hadn't been for one pompous, ill-informed, obnoxious man.

"We don't want you here!"

He materialized in front of Lynn as if her thoughts had conjured him up. Elliot Graham. A man who looked so normal, so ordinary, he might have been a mailman or a dermatologist. He stood before her, a man of average height, average build, average brown hair neatly combed. His face was an average face, unremarkable in every way except one — he had the eyes of a fanatic.

He looked self-important and self-righteous in his charcoal slacks, white shirt, burgundy tie. The epitome of the well-dressed protestor. Lynn caught a whiff of woodsy aftershave and knew instantly who had called the news crew. They were too late for the six o'clock news, but Elliot would look just as spiffy at ten. She, on the other hand, would look like a street person in her old jeans and faded T-shirt.

She closed her eyes briefly against the warning flash of pain in her right temple. As she opened them again a cameraman stepped into her line of vision, a minion behind him raising a blinding white spotlight on a long pole. Lynn flinched from the light as a reporter stepped up to her, microphone in hand.

"What do you have to say about community resentment against this move?"

"We don't want this institution in our neighborhood," Elliot Graham said emphatically, butting in front of Lynn.

"St. Stephen's Church has graciously donated the use of this house to Horizon, Mr. Graham," Lynn said, edging her way back in front of him, her hold on her temper slipping as the pain level of her headache escalated. "We intend to move in with or without your permission."

"We'll see about that."

The look on Graham's face was entirely too smug, too confident. He had an ace in the hole. Lynn braced herself mentally as she waited for him to produce it. Graham's teenage son, a budding right-wing extremist in an outfit that nearly matched his father's, stepped up and handed Graham a manila file folder from which he produced a sheaf of papers.

"Citizens for Family Neighborhoods has circulated a petition against relocating Horizon House to this property. I intend to present it to Father Bartholomew tomorrow morning. A copy will also be delivered to the bishop in Winona. We have over eight hundred signatures. . . ."

The rest of his soliloquy about quality of life and moral standards was lost on Lynn as she fought to contain her anger. Citizens for Family Neighborhoods. Good God-fearing people just trying to do what was right. She wanted to rail at them, shake them, somehow make them see that what they were doing wasn't right at all. They had no reason to fear the residents of Horizon House. Her girls weren't hardened criminals. They were just kids who needed a break, kids who needed love and understanding and acceptance.

It was clear they wouldn't find acceptance in this neighborhood, thanks to Elliot Graham and his band of vigilantes. After all the furor about their move, Lynn doubted they would find acceptance anyplace in Rochester. And there was nothing she could do about it. Nothing she could say would change their minds. In her experience, the voice of reason and truth was seldom heard above the shouts of alarmists. Her sense of impotence lodged like a hot rock behind her breastbone and her counseling skills deserted her altogether as her emotions rushed to the fore.

"You talk a good game about morals,

Mr. Graham, but you don't seem to know the first thing about kindness or charity," she snapped, the tide of passion and pain rising together and bringing a sheen of tears to blur her vision. "Do you know what you are, Mr. Graham? You're nothing but a petty, pompous —"

The news crew turned abruptly away. With the absence of light came the easing of the sword of pain, replaced by blessed cool relief. She almost collapsed as rigid muscles relaxed automatically, but her indignation held her upright. She might have finished telling Elliot Graham what she thought of him, but he had whirled away from her. Irritation pulled her brows low over her eyes. The jerk didn't even have the decency to pay attention while she told him off!

She turned to see what had so captured everyone's attention and was immediately struck in the face once again with the death strobe. Then someone stepped in front of it, blocking the worst of the light — a tall man dressed in white. The light glowed in a golden halo around his head and illuminated a pair of shoulders that belonged on a lumberjack. The effect was reminiscent of the way Hollywood portrayed holy visions. Lynn half expected to see Christ himself walk out of that aura, or Lillian's mythical white knight, Galahad come to rescue them. Fat chance.

The light shifted, coming around to illuminate his face as the news crew adjusted their positions, dancing around him like fawning spaniels. Lynn's heart did an involuntary little jump in her chest. Galahad, indeed.

State Senator Erik Gunther. Golden boy of the Democrats. Thirty-three and charming, destined for greatness, according to the media. Lynn fought a wry smile as she took in the movie-star looks of Senator Gunther, ignoring her body's physical responses to the man with the ease of long practice. She didn't have time for relationships, and she certainly had more sense than to go looking for one with a politician.

Erik Gunther might have been easy to look at, with his strong square face and dreamy blue eyes, and his boyish smile might have been enough to win the vote of every female in his district, but looks didn't make the politician. What made men like Erik Gunther was a thirst for power, a hunger for success, a drive and ambition that left room for little else. No, even if she had been interested — and she wasn't — she wouldn't have touched Erik Gunther with a ten-foot pole. She had endured enough strained and broken relationships to last her a lifetime. No sense going hunting for one.

That he wasn't here looking for a date was a cinch, anyway. He was here to get himself a cameo spot on the late news. Lynn conceded that he had a record for backing causes, but she knew how that worked. The depth of a politician's caring was in direct proportion to the amount of good it would do his image. If she was lucky, Senator Gunther would see Horizon House as being worthy of his attention long enough for her and the girls to become entrenched in this neighborhood and prove the Elliot Grahams of the town wrong.

The television reporter planted himself in front of Gunther and thrust a microphone under his nose. "Senator Gunther, can you tell us how you became involved in the dispute between Citizens for Family Neighborhoods and Horizon House?"

Lynn watched as Gunther flashed the smile that launched ten thousand ballots. The electricity that flowed out of him hit her with a jolt that almost knocked her off her feet. He was standing not more than a yard away, looking right at her, the blue of his eyes almost startling, the compassion in his expression so real she almost believed it. Amazed, she felt herself drawn to him as if he were magnetic. She had taken a step toward him before she even realized it. She pulled herself up abruptly and gave herself a mental shake. *Get ahold of yourself, Lynn. He's just a man.*

"I'm always interested when people are unjustly denied basic human rights such as housing," he said, his voice a husky baritone that somehow made him seem more like one of the people than a polished public speaker who was groomed and trained for the job.

"Then you're taking a stand against Citizens for Family Neighborhoods?"

Another smile. This one was soft, with just the perfect touch of hurt feelings. "No one is more in favor of family neighborhoods than I am."

Nice bit of fence-straddling there, Lynn thought.

"But I feel that in today's world, with one out of two marriages ending in divorce, we need to broaden our idea of what a family is. We need to look at our communities and neighborhoods as families, families that welcome new members instead of

15

shutting them out because of prejudices."

Even Elliot Graham seemed impressed by Gunther's eloquence. Graham's righteous bluster deflated like a stuck balloon. He seemed to shrink a little. Gunther had stolen his thunder and his moment on the news. He tucked his petition away in its folder and handed it back to his son. Graham Junior flashed Lynn a petulant look as if it were her fault Gunther had come to take up the gauntlet.

Lynn dismissed the boy as she scanned the crowd. The level of tension that had been building to a head as she had faced off with Graham had been cut by more than half. Whether it was the senator's words or his stunning physical presence that had done the trick, she wasn't sure, but it didn't matter. He had effectively done what she, with her many credits in psychology and counseling, had failed to do.

As her migraine took a firmer hold behind her eye, Lynn felt a stab of resentment toward Gunther. This was *her* fight. She should have been the one making the touching statements. Instead, she'd been upstaged by a golden boy and her own temper. It was the story of her life.

Gunther stepped toward her, lifted the

box of kitchen utensils out of her hands, and tucked it under one arm like a football. The spotlight hit Lynn in the face again and she flinched away from it, leaning into the senator as if she were seeking shelter and solace in the bulwark of his strength and humanitarianism. He gave her a conciliatory pat on the shoulder.

"We need to care about the youth of our nation," he said. "We need to reach out to those in trouble, not push them away. This young lady here needs our support."

Lynn's head snapped up. *Young lady?* He thought she was one of the residents! Her jaw dropped and another burst of irrational anger surged through her. He thought she was a teenager! She had been blithely discounting his prospects as a significant other while he had been looking at her and thinking she needed parental guidance!

He ended his statement with a promise to do all he could to help Horizon House. The press people thanked him and dashed off to get their stories ready in time to make deadline. The crowd of neighbors began to disperse, many heading for their homes as the streetlights began to blink on and others mingling on the lawn, chatting as the mood eased.

Erik took a deep breath and sighed, rolling his big shoulders as he took a step back from the little raven-haired beauty who was still staring up at him with a slack jaw. Teenage girls. Brother! He wouldn't have gone back to puberty for all the Twinkies in Minnesota.

He handed her her box back and flicked his thumb over a smudge of dirt on her cheek. "I know you meant well, sweetheart, but you really ought to leave Mr. Graham to the directors of the house."

She made a little strangled sound in her throat and went on staring at him, one hand clutching the box to her, the other rubbing furiously at a spot above her right eye. She was a cute little thing — maybe five-six with a wealth of black hair, bangs hanging in trendy disarray above jewel-green eyes and an impudent little nose. She choked and sputtered at him, and Erik took a cautious step toward her, concern seeping in around the edges of his appreciation for her looks.

His brows pulled together and he reached a hand toward her. "Are you all right?" Maybe she was going into a seizure or something, he thought, his heart leaping to somewhere in the vicinity of his Adam's apple. Great. The girl was having an attack just looking at him. Wonderful. He hadn't felt this special since Phoebe Heinrichs had screamed out her love for him at the National Honor Society banquet in 1976.

"Teenagers . . ." he said in a low growl as he glanced around frantically for someone who looked like a supervisor.

Two gray-haired ladies came rushing toward them from the house. A wide one wearing a Vikings jersey and sporting a face like a bulldog led the way like a blocking back, elbowing people out of their path. She was followed by a tall, slender woman who wore the unmistakable aura of a Mayo Clinic doctor's wife. Erik had met scores of them at the innumerable charity luncheons women and politicians attended in Rochester. Had he been a betting man, he would have put a fiver on her being the one who had started rattling cages in the state capital.

"Ladies." He flashed them a weak smile as he took the girl by the arm and started to usher her into their care. He'd done his duty for the night, publicly taking up the fight for Horizon House and getting himself a prime spot on the ten o'clock news. All he wanted now was a clean getaway, a steak, and a cold beer.

The girl jerked her arm free of his grasp,

upending her box of kitchen paraphernalia. Spatulas clattered on the sidewalk.
A collection of measuring cups bounced
and rolled away into the grass. Erik
turned and stared at her, truly horrified,
waiting for her head to spin around on her
shoulders.

"I am *not* a teenager," she said through
tightly gritted teeth. "I am *not* a resident of
Horizon House. I am the *counselor* of Horizon House."

He had the grace to look embarrassed.
Even in the waning light of dusk, Lynn
could see the rise of color across his perfect cheekbones.

"Oh . . . boy . . ." he said on a long,
pained sigh.

He raised his hands as if surrendering to
a thief and gave her a little smile full of
contrition and charm. Lynn steeled herself
against its full effect, yet still felt a part of
her soften toward him. It only made her
angrier. No one had a right to that much
charisma.

"I'm sorry." He gave a shrug, looking bewildered as he took in her outfit of jeans
and tattered old Notre Dame T-shirt. "I
guess you don't exactly look like my idea
of a counselor."

Lynn drew herself up to her full height

and gave him the best Ice Princess look she could muster, considering her state of dishabille. "Well, we're even, then," she said, casting a scathing glance from the white polo shirt that spanned his broad shoulders to the pale khaki chinos that hugged his slender waist, then to the Top-Siders on his feet. "You don't exactly look like my idea of a state senator, either."

Erik couldn't help but grin. She was feisty; he had to give her that. Considering the tenuous position of Horizon House, he'd expected her to beg for his help. He was in a position of power, and the people who flocked around him tended to be obsequious as a rule. It was a rule he had never liked. His job was to serve the people, not the other way around. But he got the distinct impression this lady didn't kowtow to anybody.

"You've got me there," he said. "I came straight from the golf course."

Lynn's mouth bowed into a saccharine smile. "You've had a good day, then, Senator? A few rounds on the links, drinks in the clubhouse, cap it off with a little publicity. How nice for you."

"Lynn, heel," Martha Steinbeck commanded with a warning glare. She jammed her hands where her waist would have been had she not been as wide as she was tall. Martha was sixty-five and formidable looking, with shocking red lipstick and hair the color of steel wool. "Don't pay any attention to her, Senator Gunther," she said dryly. "She had a traumatic experience with a politician as a child. It warped her."

"What happened?" he asked. His eyes, sparkling with amusement, locked on Lynn's. "She bit his hand and tasted blood?"

Lynn fought a grin without success. She didn't want to like Erik Gunther, but he was charming her just the same. Most men in his position would have been affronted by her lack of humility. Not this one. There was an unmistakable light of challenge in his eyes behind all that good humor. He was daring her to not like him, telling her he would win her over whether she wanted him to or not. "No," she said. "I bit his hand and tasted . . . something else."

Erik laughed. "I've been in politics long enough to know it's entirely possible. I'm a bona fide Type A, myself."

"That remains to be seen, doesn't it?"

He tipped his head. "Touché, counselor. I'd hate to go up against you in a debate. If

22

you could keep that temper in check, you'd probably rip me to shreds."

"I'm sorry, Senator. These days I'm afraid my temper is running on a real lean mix. It doesn't take much to touch it off." Lynn held her hand out to him in greeting and apology. "Lynn Shaw, twenty-nine, BA from the University of Minnesota. Care to check my driver's license?"

"I thought you'd say Notre Dame," he said, nodding toward the peeling gold letters on the front of her T-shirt.

"Souvenir from a past life."

Erik didn't pursue it. It seemed a harmless topic to him, but he'd seen the shutters come down on those emerald-green eyes. He had somehow managed to step over a boundary line. Intriguing lady, Miss Lynn Shaw, he thought, noting the absence of rings on her left hand. A counselor with a temper and secrets in her eyes.

He shook her hand the way he would have a colleague's hand, but he held hers just a moment longer, just to see how she would react. She didn't like it. He could feel her tension. She wanted to pull away, but she met his gaze and held firm. He added *brave* and *stubborn* to the list of adjectives that described her.

"It's nice to meet you, Miss Shaw," he said, releasing her.

"And you, Senator." Lynn broke eye contact with him, not at all comfortable with what she saw in his gaze. He was trying to read her and having too much success. "These ladies are Horizon House's founders and directors," she said, motioning to her bosses. "Martha Steinbeck and Lillian Johnson."

"Ladies," he murmured with a polite nod.

"I'm afraid you're not catching any of us at our best," Martha said. "Except Lillian. She always looks that way. Doctor's-wife syndrome."

Lillian shot her a look, then turned back to Erik: "On behalf of all of us, Senator Gunther, I want to thank you for coming to our aid."

"That's what you elected me for."

"Not me," Lynn said with a cheeky grin. "I voted for Milner."

Erik lifted a brow in sardonic amusement. "Figures."

He wanted to ask her where Mick Milner was now in her hour of need, but the question was forestalled as Elliot Graham walked up to the group.

"I feel it's only fair to warn you, Senator," he said, his face grave, his gaze locked on Erik, as if the Senator were now in charge of Horizon House. Graham's son stood beside him, arms loaded with leaflets, brows pulled low in an expression that seemed more angry than somber. The kid was maybe sixteen, gangly and on the scrawny side, Lynn noted. He had nicked his chin in two places, shaving duck fuzz. "As chairman of Citizens for Family Neighborhoods," the elder Graham went on, "I fully intend to proceed with these petitions."

Erik tucked his hands in his pockets and smiled benignly. "You do whatever you feel is right, Mr. Graham."

"It's easy for you to come in here and plead their case, Senator," Graham pointed out. "This isn't your neighborhood."

"It wouldn't make any difference if it were."

One corner of Graham's mouth flicked upward. "Have you met the residents of Horizon House yet, Senator?"

"No, I haven't."

"Meet them. Then tell me you wouldn't mind having their kind living across the street from your family."

Lynn bristled, coming to the defense of

her girls like a mother tiger for her cubs. "Just what do you mean, 'their kind'?"

Graham turned to her, looking down his nose at her with unmistakable disdain. "I think you know exactly what I mean, Miss Shaw."

She took a step toward him, her gaze locked on his face. She wanted him to say it, to put a name to what he thought of girls who had made mistakes with their lives. She wanted him to say it so she could feel justified in slapping that holier-than-thou look off his face. But it wasn't Elliot Graham who cooperated. It was his son.

"Sluts."

The word was barely spoken aloud, just a whisper of sound, but it brought Lynn up short. The venom in it shocked her. Young Graham's cheeks colored as all eyes turned toward him. His father wheeled on him with a furious look.

"E.J.!" he barked.

The boy gaped at him. "But, Dad —"

"We're going home," Graham said in a tight, low voice that boded ill for his son. He grabbed the boy by one arm and steered him roughly toward the side-walk.

An itchy silence descended on the group

as they stood watching the Grahams hustle across the street.

"My God," Lillian muttered, her voice laced with disgust.

Martha just shook her head.

Erik was more interested in watching Lynn than the Grahams. The boy's remark had upset her in a way that seemed out of proportion to the situation. The color her temper had brought to her face had washed out, leaving her pale. She covered it admirably by rubbing her forehead as if to shield her eyes, then made an acerbic comment to divert attention from herself.

"I'll bet he has to do extra pages in his Hitler Youth workbook tonight."

"Are you all right?"

Her head jerked up and she stared at him as if he'd just asked her how she liked her sex. "I'm fine," she said too quickly. "I have a little headache. It's nothing."

Martha rolled her eyes. "Like being hit with a sledge-hammer is nothing."

"I'm fine," Lynn repeated in a tone that declared the subject closed.

She'd lived with migraines for twenty years. She knew the routine by now. This one hadn't decided whether it would stay or not. If she got some medication into her system quickly enough, she would be all right. If she didn't, she would be violently ill and unable to function for a few hours. Either way, she didn't much care for Erik Gunther to know about her problem. She didn't want him getting any closer than an emotional arm's length away. He was here for his own reasons, and when he left he wouldn't be taking any part of her with him.

"Thank you again for dropping by, Senator," she said, kneeling to gather up the utensils. The quicker they gave Gunther enough praise to bask in and allowed him to make his obligatory promises, the quicker he'd be gone. The quicker he was gone, the quicker she would be safe from those all-seeing blue eyes of his. "We appreciate whatever support you can give us."

"I'll help any way I can," Erik said.

He dropped to one knee on the cracked pavement and reached for a spaghetti spoon, his fingers brushing over Lynn's as she drew her hand away. She gave him a good poker face, but her eyes betrayed her. They watched him with a kind of caution in their depths that only served to intrigue him more. The lady was trying to give him the brush-off. She was in retreat mode.

And yet there was the faint, but unmistakable, crackle of attraction in the air between them. The contradiction was irresistible to him.

A slow smile spread across his face. *You're not getting rid of me yet, Miss Shaw.* He lifted the spoon and tapped it against his chest. "I live to serve."

Her eyes watchful, she reached out for the spoon and snatched it away when he offered it, like a wild creature venturing near enough to accept a treat but not near enough to be touched. "I'll bear that in mind."

"Maybe we could discuss it in more detail. Say, over dinner?"

Lynn shook her head, "I don't think —"

"Great idea, Senator!" Martha bellowed, ignoring the murderous glare Lynn shot her. "The Mongolian beef is on the way. We can all sit down and have a chat."

"Maybe the senator doesn't like Mongolian beef," Lynn said tightly.

"The senator would eat an old boot with catsup right about now." Erik pushed himself to his feet and held a hand out for Lynn. "How about it, counselor? Break fortune cookies with me?"

Lynn arched a brow. "Do I have a choice?"

"Do you really want one?" he challenged softly.

Martha and Lillian had already started for the house. No witnesses. Not that they had been any help while they'd been standing there, Lynn thought. They had seemed impervious to the undercurrents, to the subtle ritual of male advance and female retreat that had been going on right in front of them.

She looked up at Erik Gunther, Lillian's white knight, and wondered just how tarnished that armor of his might be underneath that beautiful facade. He had a spotless record, but she was too worldly-wise to go by that. Politics was a game of favor-trading. Just what favors would Senator Gunther expect for helping her? She didn't want to find out, but the truth was, she needed his help more than she needed to be rid of him. The old adage about politics making strange bedfellows drifted through her mind, and Lynn pushed it aside, ignoring both the image it conjured and the unwelcome wash of heat that came with it.

Disregarding Erik's hand, she rose, clutching her kitchen utensils to her chest. "I guess I'll take my chances, Senator."

He gave her a slow smile that seemed

wise and warm, as if he alone held the answer to one of life's great secrets, and Lynn felt her heart roll over in her chest like a trick poodle as he said, "I guess we both will, Counselor Shaw."

# — 2 —

"So, where are your residents?" Erik asked as he set his plate aside. He addressed the question to no one in particular, but his gaze fell on Lynn.

They sat at opposite ends of the coffee table in matching country-blue overstuffed chairs. Lynn picked at a grain of rice on her plate, fighting the urge to rub her head. The medication she had taken was keeping her migraine in check, but Erik Gunther's presence kept it from disappearing altogether. The knot of pain throbbed dully above her eye. The sexual tension in the room seemed a palpable thing to her, but Lillian and Martha, ensconced on the sofa together, seemed oblivious to it.

"They're back at the other house," Martha said, scanning the contents of the small white boxes on the coffee table. She selected snow peas and mushrooms and deposited a heap of it on her plate.

Erik lifted a brow, his gaze still on Lynn, as if he thought he might will her to speak to him. "Unsupervised? Is that wise?"

Graham's remark about "their kind" was

still too fresh in Lynn's mind for her not to react. She straightened a little in her chair and gave him a cool look. "Horizon House is a home, Senator, not a prison. We don't keep the girls under watch twenty-four hours a day."

He didn't flinch. His gaze remained steady, warm, searching, curious, trying to find a way beneath her armor even while he kept the conversation to the topic at hand. "I think with all the controversy you're generating it might be prudent to make an exception to that rule. Purely precautionary, you know."

"Cover our tails?" Lynn said dryly.

He smiled that soft little secretive smile that hinted at amusement and wisdom. "So to speak. Imagine what might happen if some of Graham's demonstrators decided to set up a picket line outside the other house. It could be a very unpleasant situation for your girls and a potential public relations nightmare for the home."

"Well, no one would know more about looking good to the public than a politician."

"Senator Gunther makes an excellent point, Lynn," Lillian said with a note of censure in her voice. "It's important for the girls to know we trust them, but the stakes are too high for us to take chances right now."

The argument was logical and practical. Lynn probably would have made it herself if Erik Gunther hadn't come up with it first. She simply didn't like having him intrude on her territory — not in the physical sense, not in the psychological sense. She was tired and frustrated and in pain, and every feminine warning system she had was on red alert. The combination tended to make her snappish.

She could feel Gunther's eyes on her, looking for things she didn't want to reveal, and her instinctive response was to run. But she wouldn't do that. She had spent enough of her life running to know it never solved anything. Besides, the watchfulness of the senator's gaze reminded her too much of a wolf. She had the unnerving feeling that if she ran he would automatically give chase.

"Lillian will be taking me back to the other house," Martha said calmly. "I'll be staying the night there while Lynn keeps watch over our stuff here. I think the girls will be all right until after I've finished my tea."

Erik nodded. "You're probably right, Mrs. Steinbeck. Graham's people didn't seem too fired up when they left here."

"Thanks to you, Senator." She lifted her teacup in salute. "And call me Martha. I haven't been Mrs. Steinbeck in such a long time I probably won't answer to it."

"All right, Martha." Erik nodded. "And I'd like it if you would all call me Erik. I'm not much for standing on ceremony with friends."

Lillian and Martha beamed smiles at him. Lynn watched him, her gaze steady and slightly wary, like a she-wolf who was too intelligent to turn down his help but was not about to drop her guard and let him get too near. Erik wondered where she had come by that much caution, wondered if it was politicians in general she didn't trust or him in particular.

"What do you think our chances are for staying here, Erik?" Lillian asked.

Tearing his thoughts and his gaze away from Lynn, he took a sip of his tea and set the dainty cup down on its saucer on the coffee table. "Hard to call. It'll depend on how tenacious Graham's group is, and how shrewd. They've promised to put pressure on the church. They could try for an injunction against you, demand a community viability study, but they should have done that before now. The nearer you are to actually residing here, the less likely a judge is to prevent you from moving in." His gaze skimmed the living room and the hall beyond, taking in a fair amount of furniture and boxes piled in precarious-looking stacks. The old house still had an empty feeling to it with its blank white walls, but it wasn't far from being made into a home. "They can't challenge you on any zoning ordinance. They can call for a new ordinance against group homes of this type in residential neighborhoods, but even if they succeeded with that, they couldn't touch you. An ordinance of that type only applies to what happens after it goes on the books."

"You've done your homework, Senator," Lynn murmured.

Erik met her gaze, letting her know without saying a word that he'd caught her deliberate use of his title. He had taken that boundary away; Lynn had put it back. He let it be for the moment.

"I'm interested in more than just getting my picture taken while supporting a cause," he said evenly. "I wouldn't have come here tonight without knowing all the facts."

"I thought you said you came here from the golf course."

He flashed her a grin. "I may insist on fighting my own battles, but I don't have any trouble asking my staff to do the legwork."

She conceded the point with a tip of her head, then went back to the real issue. "If Graham's group has no legal recourse other than getting the church to kick us out, then are we home free?"

"No. They can make it so unpleasant for you to live here that you'll want to leave." Erik leaned forward and settled his forearms on his thighs, hands dangling between his knees. "From what I saw tonight, that's a real possibility."

Lynn put her plate down, her meal virtually untouched. One winged brow lifted. "Isn't that called harassment?"

"Not as long as they have a permit to demonstrate and don't trespass on private property or break any laws," Erik said, thinking she would have made a great queen with that look. "Democracy is a great system but it can be a real pain in the fanny sometimes. Graham and his followers are entitled to freedom of speech. You may not like or agree with anything they say, but you can't stop them from saying it unless it's slanderous."

*Sluts.* The word came back to Lynn like

a memory from a bad dream. Erik Gunther's face faded from view as images of the crowd on the lawn came back to her. She knew what it was like to feel unwanted, unwelcome. So did her girls. Their faith in humanity wasn't going to be restored if they were subjected to that kind of ridicule day after day. And that was what her job was all about — restoring their faith in people, making them feel welcome and loved, coaxing them back into the mainstream before they became so alienated they could never fit in. But people like Elliot Graham stood in her way, spreading venom to everyone around him until she and her girls were surrounded by a moat of it, more isolated than ever.

"Well, nothing else is going to happen tonight," Lillian declared. Lynn started from her trance, catching the worry in her boss's eyes. Lillian may have liked to play the cool sophisticate, but inside she was marshmallow — a mother hen with swan's plumage. Even as she addressed herself to their guest, she couldn't seem to stop herself from patting Lynn's hand, which gripped the arm of the chair. "And we have no way of knowing the future, so we might as well not worry ourselves too much before the fact."

"Maybe we can see the future in the senator's tea leaves," Martha said with a wry smile. She hefted herself forward on the couch and reached for Erik's cup.

He looked at her with skeptical surprise. "You read tea leaves?"

Lynn fought a chuckle. He was obviously struggling with the idea, too polite to scoff outright, too staid to believe. She liked seeing him off balance. It tempered those Norse-god looks of his with a little human frailty.

"Our Martha is a woman of many varied and weird interests," she said. "Ask her to read the bumps on your head sometime."

"Maybe when we know each other a little better," he suggested, shifting in his chair as if the mere mention of this kind of thing made him physically uncomfortable. Still, he watched with interest as Martha swirled the last of the tea in his cup, then poured the liquid into the saucer. She set the cup down on the table and stared down into it, frowning like a bulldog. Cautiously, Erik leaned over and peered into the china, then cast an expectant look at Martha. She smiled like a medium who had just heard a joke from someone on the other side.

"Well," she said, "I don't know about the

rest of us, but your future looks interesting, Erik."

Erik sat on the edge of his seat, poised to hear the details. Martha dismissed the subject, planted her hands on her knees, and rocked herself to her feet.

"I'd better get back to the house. Come along, Lillian."

"But — but you didn't tell me —" Erik rose to his feet, looking bewildered.

Martha waved a plump hand at him. "Oh, that would take all the fun out of it, now, wouldn't it?"

"But —"

"Don't worry, Senator," Lynn said as she pushed herself out of her chair. "She'd tell you if you were in danger of being hit by a bus."

They all made their way into the front hall. Lillian pulled her keys out of her purse. Martha stood on tiptoe to give Lynn a kiss on the cheek.

"We'll see you in the morning, sweetheart. Have a good night."

"It's been swell so far," Lynn said sarcastically.

Martha took her by the arms, her round face suddenly a study in seriousness. "Make lemonade," she said clearly.

Lynn blinked at her.

She repeated the line as if it were a vital piece of coded information. "Make lemonade. When life gives you lemons, make lemonade. Something good will come of this. You'll see."

"Thank you again, Erik," Lillian said as she swung the door open. "I'm glad we had the chance to meet. Perhaps we can all get together sometime tomorrow and discuss strategy."

"Yes, that sounds fine."

The ladies said their good-byes and headed down the sidewalk toward Lillian's Volvo. Lynn stood holding the front door open, watching until they had gotten safely to the car and started the engine.

Night had fallen on the neighborhood, velvet black and quiet. Lights glowed amber in windows up and down the block, but there were no signs of life outside. Still, Lynn thought she sensed something, something heavy and taut in the darkness. A sense of tension, a malevolence, as if someone were standing in the shadows staring at her.

It was just her own anxiety, she told herself as one of the neighborhood dogs loped across the yard with a big grin on his face. She was tired and edgy and felt a little abandoned as Martha and Lillian drove off into the night. Abandoned, but not alone.

She turned toward Erik Gunther as she pulled the door closed against the swarm of moths and mosquitoes that had flocked to the porch light. He was standing just a little too close, watching her just a little too intently. He looked perfectly relaxed, standing there with his hands tucked into the pockets of his chinos, one leg cocked, but she sensed the power in him, the magnetism, the energy. He seemed very, very male, and that made her nervous. It also made her acutely aware of how long it had been since she'd been conscious of a man in the sexual sense. Ages. Eons. Her body hadn't forgotten how to react, however. As warm tingles danced through her, she couldn't decide if that was good news or bad.

Hand still gripping the doorknob, she tried to look the part of a hostess bidding a guest good night. "Thank you for dropping by, Senator."

"Giving me the bum's rush, Counselor Shaw?" he asked, blue eyes sparkling like sapphires under the hall light. "We haven't opened our fortune cookies yet. Maybe mine will tell me what Martha wouldn't."

He didn't give her a chance to say no, turning and sauntering back into the living

42

room as if he had all the time in the world. Lynn heaved a weary sigh and gave in, rubbing at the knot of tension and pain above her eye.

"What you need is someone to do that for you."

She jerked her head up, startled to see he had turned around and was leaning against the living room doorway watching her.

"I took a course in massage when I was playing college football," he said. "You can't fully release tension when you're actively generating energy."

"I'll bear that in mind."

"Care for a demonstration?" He raised his hands, fingers splayed wide, like a surgeon waiting for his gloves to be put on. "I'm pretty good with my hands."

"I don't doubt it," Lynn muttered. She stepped around him and went into the living room, where she began gathering up the supper dishes with efficiency.

Erik hung back for a moment, admiring the fit of her jeans as she bent over the low table. She had a slim, angular build, but her backside was nicely rounded, inviting a man to touch. The old jeans hugged her lovingly, giving a faint, tantalizing glimpse of black lace panties where the denim had worn thin beneath one pocket. Desire stirred, warm and silky, in his groin.

"Let me help you with that," he said as she straightened.

"You don't have to."

"My mother raised me better than that. You fed me, I help clean up."

He didn't allow her to protest, but took the stack of plates from her and headed out of the room in search of the kitchen. Lynn followed like a woman resigned to her own execution, the tray of take-out boxes held before her like the remains of her final meal.

In the kitchen the sink was already filling with water and soap bubbles. Erik had set the plates aside and was busy snooping through drawers. He pulled out a dishcloth and a cotton towel.

"You wash, I'll dry," he said.

"Afraid of being seen in an apron?" Lynn asked dryly. She dumped the cartons in the garbage and set the tray on the counter beside the dishes.

"Naw," he drawled, handing her the dishcloth. "Voters understand aprons. They like the new Nineties Man image. It's ladies' underwear they frown on."

Lynn couldn't help the little cough of laughter. She would have pegged Erik Gunther as a man who took himself too se-

44

riously. That he had a sense of humor was a nice surprise.

"I don't know," she said, giving him a sidelong look as she sank her hands into the warm suds. "You might look kind of cute in a garter belt. You could attract a whole new demographic group."

"And a lot of weird phone calls."

"It could open new vistas in your personal life."

"I like the vistas I have right now just fine, thanks."

They worked in silence for a few moments, but it was hardly a companionable silence. Lynn was too aware of him standing beside her, and too aware of her desire to like him. He was here to help, she reminded herself, but he had his own agenda and his own goals. It just wouldn't do for her to like him too much.

"I don't bite," he said softly. Lynn started and looked up at him, wide-eyed. A rakish smile tugged at one corner of his mouth and he waggled his eyebrows. "Unless it's a specific request, that is."

"I was just . . . thinking about Elliot Graham," she lied, turning her attention back to the dishes.

Erik's face crumpled. "Oh." He pulled a plate out of the rinse water and dried it slowly. "Haven't you had enough of him for one night?"

Lynn sniffed. "I've had enough of him to last me forever, but I can't just ignore him. The man is the bane of my existence."

Erik heaved a sigh. "I know he's pompous and somewhere to the right of Mussolini, politically speaking, but I do think he means well, if that's any consolation."

"Not much. As they say, the road to hell is paved with good intentions." Lynn washed another plate methodically, the warm water beginning to soothe her jangled nerves. She relaxed with the change of topic, too, much more comfortable discussing issues than experiencing those intangible sexual vibrations. "If he would look past his own self-righteousness, he might see just how wrong he is. But that will never happen. The man is so narrow-minded his ears rub together."

"He's a man with a cause," Erik said. "I see it all the time. He's got the bit in his teeth and blinkers on to keep his mind on his purpose. He doesn't want to be swayed by anything like the possibility that he's wrong."

"He's so wrong. The irony of it is that it's attitudes like Graham's that help foster problems like the ones my girls have."

He gave a snort of disbelief. "You're saying they all have fathers like Graham and that's why they grow up to be bad girls? That's a little simplistic, isn't it?"

"I resent the term 'bad girls.' And what would you know about it, anyway?" Lynn queried defensively, turning to face him. She propped her right hand on her hip, ignoring the soap suds that soaked into her T-shirt. An old resentment seeped out of its hiding place and directed itself at the man before her — Sir Erik the Good, golden boy, favored son, everybody's hero. He was the male version of her sister Rebecca, bright and perfect, loved by all. "I'll bet your father was your best pal. You played football together. He took you fishing and supported you in everything you did. Right?"

His expression suddenly went closed, but the residue of pain glowed in his eyes, and Lynn had the feeling she'd just taken one giant step onto private property.

"My dad died when I was sixteen," he said quietly.

Damn. Lynn wanted to say she was sorry, but she couldn't seem to speak around the foot in her mouth. It was this kind of thing that had gotten her in trouble with teachers and supervisors over the years. Her lack of reserve and circumspection made her good with teenagers but a failure with most adults. She looked at Erik and felt helpless.

"He played football with me," he said. "He took me fishing. He supported me in everything I did. And then he dropped dead of a heart attack, leaving a wife, five kids, and a stack of bills."

Shame crawled around in Lynn's stomach like a whipped dog. She didn't usually judge people so quickly and on so little evidence. She had labeled Erik Gunther the product of a privileged upbringing, handsome, successful, shallow. Slapping an unattractive label on him was a defense mechanism, she supposed, trying to keep him a safe distance away, but that didn't make it right.

"I'm sorry," she said at last.

"Yeah, well . . ."

He turned away and scooped a handful of silverware out of the sink, then went in search of the proper drawer. Lynn watched him, her eyes on the set of his broad shoulders. He kept his head down, ostensibly concentrating on his work as he sorted the forks and spoons. She wanted to reach out to him, to heal the hurt she'd inflicted by opening an old scar, and because she wanted to do that, she turned away. Erik Gunther wasn't one of her girls. He was a grown man, fully capable of dealing with his own feelings. If she reached out to him, she would be the one in trouble.

She turned back to the sink and lifted the drain basket to let the water out. As the suds were sucked down, she stared out the window above the sink, seeing nothing but blackness and her own reflection, like a ghost. Her thoughts drifted inexorably back to her own unhappy youth.

"I lost my mother when I was eleven," she said absently, her concentration on the memory.

Lovely Gabrielle with her gentleness and patience, taken an excruciating bit at a time by ALS — Lou Gehrig's disease. A disease named for a baseball player, as if it were his exclusively. Her mother, the only person who had ever really understood her, gone, abandoning her for death, leaving her to a father who demanded perfection even from the mediocre. The emotions she had known nearly two decades ago bubbled up anew, and Lynn tamped them back into their little box and shut the lid.

When she turned, Erik was looking at

her, studying her again. She wondered how much he had seen, but she was too tired to care. He seemed too close again, his big frame out of place in the narrow confines of the kitchen.

"You've done your duty," she said, one hand fluttering toward the empty sink. "You're free to go."

"Why do I get the impression you want me out of here?" he asked with a chuckle, her abrupt change in attitude amusing him.

Lynn shrugged and gave him a phony grin. "Gee, I don't know. Maybe it's because I want you out of here. It's been a long day. I'd like to take my headache and go to bed."

Erik made a pained face. "Ouch. Passed over for a headache. I must be losing my touch."

"I wouldn't worry about it if I were you," Lynn said dryly. "I'm sure there are plenty of women out there ready to cast their votes for you, Senator."

"But you're not one of them, right?"

"I don't mix business with my personal life." She didn't have a personal life, but that was beside the point. This wasn't the time to start one — or the man to do it with.

He took a step closer, closing the distance between them by half. Lynn had to tip her head back to maintain eye contact with him. He tilted his head a little to one side, as if he were studying a modern sculpture and trying to discern whether it was right side up or not. His eyes were narrowed in speculation. Strands of golden hair tumbled across his forehead.

"That's a very convenient rule," he said at last.

"It's a very practical rule," Lynn countered.

"But you don't strike me as a very practical woman."

"Thanks," she said with an incredulous laugh. She used affront as an excuse to take a step back from him, to try to escape his scrutiny.

"You've got too much fire, too much spirit," he said bluntly. "Why do you bottle it up when it comes to your personal life?"

"That's my business."

"For the moment."

Lynn's heart gave a lurch. "What's that supposed to mean?"

He smiled again, warm and friendly in the face of her suspicion. "It means I'd like to get to know you better."

She shook her head. "I don't think that's a very good idea."

"Why not?"

There were a dozen reasons why not. Because she didn't allow room in her life for casual relationships with men. Because she wouldn't allow a transient figure in her life to get close to her. Because she knew he didn't *really* want to know her, wouldn't want to know a woman with a past that might tarnish that shining armor of his, wouldn't run that kind of risk to his image. Because she had too good an idea of what he was after — a little publicity, with some extracurricular fun thrown in, to make all this trouble worth his while.

There were a dozen reasons she could have listed, but for once she gave the prudent answer instead of speaking her mind. "There's too much possibility for conflict of interest."

Erik nodded slowly, sagely, all the while thinking *bull hooey.* He knew political rhetoric when he heard it: pat, broad, with enough of the truth to make it difficult for rebuttal. She had put on her mask of cool reserve, subdued her gestures, gone into retreat again. Like a possum playing dead until the predator lost interest and wandered away. Only she was a darn sight

52

prettier than any possum he'd ever encountered. She stood there with her back to the sink, her hands folded primly in front of her, gaze steady. She was so still, the pulse beating in her throat was about the only thing that confirmed she was a living creature and not just some figment of his imagination.

Of course she was real. His imagination had never conjured up a woman this intriguing, or this hard to win over.

He crossed his arms over his chest in a relaxed pose and went instinctively for the nerve that would bring Ms. Shaw out of her shell. "What are you afraid of?"

Fire flashed instantly in her eyes. The lush, tempting little mouth thinned to a tight line. Color blushed across her cheekbones. Her hands knotted together as if each was keeping the other from gesticulating. "Nothing." She bit the word off. "I'm not afraid of anything."

Erik ignored her denial and pressed a little harder on that raw nerve, willing her to come to life for him. "Afraid we might actually like each other? Afraid I might get a peek behind that armor of yours?"

Her slender shoulders were rigid with the anger she was so visibly fighting to contain. She crossed her arms tightly against herself, but took an aggressive step forward and tilted her square little chin to a sassy angle.

"I'm not afraid of anything, Senator," she snapped, glaring up at him, eyes glowing like emeralds in the sun. "I don't like being pressured and I don't like being used. If it's a prostitute you're looking for, I'm sure you can find one. Even a Camelot like Rochester has hookers."

Her statement took him completely by surprise, a sucker punch out of nowhere. Erik shook his head a little, as if the blow had stunned him. He took a half-step back from her, dropping his hands to the waistband of his slacks. "What the hell is that supposed to mean?"

"Oh, come on, Senator," Lynn sneered, letting her temper run off unchecked. She let go of herself emotionally and physically, her hands springing free. "I'm not naive. You want a few perks for your trouble. You scratch my back, I scratch your libido, right? Well, I'm sorry, but I won't play that game."

Erik pulled back abruptly. He was a man who lived by what was perhaps an outdated code of honor, a man of his word, a man of integrity. The idea of a woman accusing him of something so low, so disgusting as sexual extortion was incomprehensible to him.

He curled his hands into fists to keep from grabbing Lynn Shaw and shaking her until her teeth rattled. The anger that roared through him was enough to take his breath away. He stomped around the kitchen, turning back toward her twice and turning away again, still too furious to speak. He tried to tell himself he'd asked for it, prodding and pushing her to get a reaction, but that didn't assuage his ego any. He had, after all, come here out of the goodness of his heart to save her, and this was the thanks he got!

Finally, his temper erupted and he simply wheeled on her, backing her toward the counter.

"I don't play games, Ms. Shaw," he said through clenched teeth, his voice as tight as piano wire. "I don't expect sexual favors. Not to brag, but I hardly need to blackmail women to get them into my bed. I'm here because I believe in your cause. I'd be here if you were a frumpy little toad of a woman with B.O. and a big hairy wart on your chin.

"But the cause has nothing to do with what goes on between us," he whispered, leaning down close, hands braced on the counter on either side of her. "Do you understand me? What goes on between us — *if* anything goes on between us — has nothing to do with politics or Horizon House. It has to do with *us.* You and me. A woman and a man. Is that clear?"

Lynn stared up at him, her eyes as wide as twin moons. Her heart was thumping like a trip-hammer in her chest. He was no more than a deep breath away, the scant space between them hot and electric with tension. His chest was heaving with the exertion of his outburst, nearly touching her with every inhalation. She leaned back harder against the countertop, the metal molding strip biting into her back.

He didn't seem like the kind of man to lose his temper. She'd have taken him for the type to hang on to his emotions, never swinging too far one way or the other, always maintaining that sterling image. But she'd struck a nerve — two in one night, lucky her — and the calm, perfect facade had cracked to reveal a real man. She would have congratulated herself if this had been her office and she had been struggling for a breakthrough with him as a patient. Only he wasn't a patient, and she was pretty sure she didn't want to know what the man beneath the image was like.

She didn't want anything to do with him at all.

"Have I made myself understood, Ms. Shaw?" Erik asked again.

On one plane of awareness it occurred to him that this entire scene was somehow out of sync and out of character. They had only just met. But from the moment he had realized she wasn't a juvenile delinquent, he had felt himself drawn to her, the way males had been drawn to females since time immemorial. They had been skirting the issue of attraction all night, circling around it like two cats wrangling for a tussle, feeling each other out in subtle ways. It seemed imperative that she understand now, before they knew each other a minute longer, that this electricity between them had nothing to do with anything except nature.

He stared down at her, taking in the luminous green eyes that were fringed by thick, sooty lashes, the slim retroussé nose, the delicately carved cheekbones. Her skin was pale, a rose-and-cream hue that looked so soft his fingertips itched to caress it. And her mouth, oh, her mouth . . . It was naturally sultry, naturally pouty, not too wide but perfectly sculpted. Her lips were slightly parted now as she watched him, her breath slipping between them in shallow puffs.

The ground seemed to shift slowly beneath his feet. The air around them grew dense and warm. Thoughts of their argument, of Horizon House, of everything else in the world spun away, allowing his mind to focus on one idea — he wanted to kiss her.

Lynn saw it coming in the darkening of his eyes. She felt it coming as he leaned even closer, his head slowly ducking down toward hers. She felt it within herself, in the tingling of her breasts and the sudden sweet ache in the pit of her belly. She told herself this was the last thing she wanted, but she made no move to prevent it from happening.

His lips brushed across hers in a gentle, testing kiss, a preliminary phase that allowed her to end it there if she wanted. He pulled back slightly, his gaze, hooded and liquid blue, searching hers, silently asking permission. For the life of her, Lynn didn't know what her answer would be, but it didn't matter, because she never got the chance to give it.

The glass in the window behind her suddenly exploded, shards flying into the room like crystal daggers. Time fragmented along with the glass, seeming swift and slow at once. Instinctively, Lynn flinched, but she didn't scream. Her brain couldn't seem to assimilate the events taking place. All messages stalled out, shocked to a halt. The next thing she knew, she was on the floor, pinned to the linoleum by the solid masculine weight of Erik Gunther.

# — 3 —

The silence that came in its wake was nearly as deafening as the crash had been. For an instant, absolute stillness pressed in on Lynn's ears. Then she became aware of the sound of her blood rushing in her head, her breath coming in ragged gasps. She turned her head away from the smothering warmth of Erik's shoulder, her gaze taking in the broken glass scattered, jagged and glittering, on the kitchen floor. Still unable to comprehend what had just happened, she tried to rise, her mind latching on to the idea that she should get a broom and clean up the mess.

Erik held her in place with his body. "Stay down," he whispered. His breath was coming hard and fast. He twisted his head around to glimpse the damage, cursing under his breath. The light switch was on the other side of the room, right next to the telephone. There was no getting to either one without either crawling across a bed of broken glass or becoming a moving target in front of the window.

"What was it?" Lynn asked, finally

shaking off the astonishment. "A bullet? Is somebody shooting at us?"

"I don't know. It happened too fast." He propped himself up on his elbows and looked down at her, concern knitting his brows. "Are you all right?"

The question struck Lynn as absurd. She was flat on her back on the linoleum with the political hunk of the year sprawled on top of her. Her legs were sandwiched between his, her belly pressed to his belly. There was certainly no question of his gender; the proof was nudging her in a very sensitive spot. Sexual heat mingled with the adrenaline surging through her veins, making her feel vaguely dizzy.

"I'll be fine as soon as you get off me," she said, covering her anxiety with annoyance.

Erik eased himself off her carefully, turning to crouch beside the cupboard. Lynn pushed herself up into a sitting position with her back against the cabinet door. The only sounds that came in through the broken window were night sounds — the distant bark of a dog, someone's television mumbling through an open window, a car driving past in the street — no shots, no voices, no footsteps in retreat. A gray rock the size of a tennis ball lay on the floor by the refrigerator. There was an ugly dent in the refrigerator door at about head height. The impact had taken out a scab of white paint, leaving a gray spot in the center of the indentation.

Lynn muttered a curse. "That's just great. Now we've got to pay for a new refrigerator door."

"You could be paying for neurosurgery," Erik said. "That had to have damn near hit you in the head."

An involuntary shudder skittered down Lynn's back. "Nice neighborhood. Instead of a welcoming committee they send out stoning brigades. Charming people."

"I'm calling the cops," Erik said decisively, moving in a crouch along the cupboard toward the other side of the room.

"What for?" Lynn stood up and began dusting herself off, trying to brush away the lingering feel of his body against hers. "They'll take one look, tell us it's a rock, and leave."

Erik straightened, frowning, irked by her attitude. "We can't let a crime go unreported."

Lynn said nothing. She had an aversion to men in uniforms that dated back to her days as a juvenile offender, when she'd gone through a pattern of destructive behavior to get her father's attention — shoplifting, skipping school, drinking . . . the kind of things guaranteed to raise a Notre Dame professor's ire, if nothing else. Her experiences with law enforcement had not been happy ones, but she said nothing as Erik lifted the receiver from its cradle and punched 911. She had a feeling he wouldn't understand, any more than her father had.

He was a straight arrow, Senator Gunther. Even more so than she had first imagined, if his righteous anger over her insinuation about his motives was anything to go by. Upholder of laws, defender of good. He had to be the last white knight on earth. And she had to be the last woman he would want anything to do with. He just didn't know it yet.

"It's a rock."

Erik scowled as he caught the "I told you so" look Lynn rolled his way. "We know it's a rock, Officer Reuter. What do you intend to do about it?"

The cop heaved a weary sigh, as if he had been asked to explain the theory of relativity in twenty words or less. He was a short, stocky man in his forties with just a little too much middle for his fitted uni-

form shirt. He scratched his pocket note-
book back through his mop of curly red
hair. "We'll take it with us as evidence.
Dust it for prints."

His partner came in through the kitchen
door, a tall, slim man with a Dennis
Weaver mustache. "I didn't see anybody. It
was probably just some kid screwing
around. Too bad about the fridge."

They stayed for another twenty minutes,
going through the motions of taking statements, doing what they could to soothe
Erik's temper. Lynn hung back out of their
way, rubbing at the ache that had broken
through the haze of her medication. Unless
they came back to ingratiate themselves
with Erik by feigning diligence, this would
be the last she'd see of Officers Reuter and
Briggs. No one had seen the perpetrator.
There was no realistic hope of catching
whoever had launched that fastball
through the window.

Father Bartholomew, the priest who had
offered the use of the house to Horizon,
came over from the rectory to express his
concern and to cast pained looks at the
dented refrigerator. He was a small man in
his fifties with kind, dark eyes and a general aura of dishevelment. His clothes were
always slightly rumpled, his thinning dark

hair never quite in place, glasses forever askew. He had the pointed face and bright, anxious look of a cartoon mouse.

Lynn knew he had gone out on a limb offering them the use of the house, and she felt terrible that his kindness had brought him so much trouble. Bravery wasn't something that came easily to Father Bartholomew. She wished he could have been rewarded for his effort instead of ridiculed. She told him as much as they stood paying their respects to the disfigured refrigerator.

He flashed her a preoccupied little smile. "Our rewards are greater in heaven than on earth, Lynn. Oh, my, yes." He reached a finger out toward the dent, but pulled up abruptly, as if he were afraid to touch it, and pushed his round-rimmed glasses up on his nose instead.

"That won't take much," Lynn muttered. "From what I've seen in this life, no good deed goes unpunished."

Father Bartholomew clicked his tongue like an angry squirrel, his face awash in disappointment. He looked ready to admonish her for her pessimism, but was distracted as Officer Reuter bent over to pick up the rock with a kitchen tongs. The priest went a little pale and backed away, his thick-soled shoes crunching on the broken glass.

"Angels in heaven," he mumbled, crossing himself. "Thank goodness no one was hurt." His gaze darted anxiously to Lynn. "You're certain you're not hurt?" As she nodded, his head swiveled toward Erik. "Senator?"

"I'm fine, Father."

"Thank goodness." The little priest wagged his head in dismay. "I don't want to know what the bishop will have to say about this. He can be a real tiger, I can tell you."

Lynn was more curious about what the bishop would say to Elliot Graham's petition, but she held her tongue, not wanting to upset Father Bartholomew any more.

He left with the police, who were carrying the offending rock in a plastic sandwich bag like an item for show-and-tell at school. Lynn stood at the front door and watched them go, her gaze reaching out beyond them to the neighboring houses, where people peered out windows and doors. The patrol car sat at the curb with its lights flashing like an oversize Christmas toy, a beacon to herald trouble. In her state of exhaustion and frustration, she could imagine the neighbors were staring right past the car, directing malevolent looks at her, as if it were her fault someone had vandalized the house, as if no one had ever before had to call the police in this fine, upstanding neighborhood.

She slowly stepped back inside and turned toward Erik. He looked tired and disappointed that his precious system of jurisprudence had let him down. It was all Lynn could do to keep herself from giving him a conciliatory hug.

"Now that you've done your civic duty, Senator," she said dryly, "can we call it a night?"

He stuffed his hands in his pockets and sighed, shoulders sagging. "Yeah, let's call it a night. Where do you want me to bed down?"

The question hit Lynn square in the chest, jolting the breath from her. She looked at him with a careful poker face, hoping to heaven she'd heard him wrong. "In your own little bed across town, or wherever it is you live," she said evenly.

Erik shook his head. "Uh-uh. You could have been hurt tonight. I'm not going anywhere."

Lynn gaped at him, incredulous. "Well, you're not staying here!"

"Guess again, counselor." He planted

himself in the doorway to the living room, feet spread, back against the door frame, looking for all the world like the original immovable object.

"You can't stay here with me," Lynn argued vehemently. "My God, what if the press got hold of that?"

"Someone attacked this house tonight and may very well have meant to attack you personally. What kind of man would I be if I just said 'so long' and went home?"

"The kind who has a healthy respect for gossipmongers."

"I don't have any respect for gossipmongers. I'm staying here to protect you. It's perfectly innocent."

"Famous last words," Lynn muttered, pacing the hall, her sneakers squeaking on the hardwood floor, her right hand rubbing anxiously at her forehead. " 'It was perfectly innocent.' That's what Gary Hart said. One day he's running for president, the next he's sitting in an office somewhere making paper-clip chains."

Erik stepped out to block her path, taking hold of her shoulders. He looked her in the eyes, his expression curiously sweet. "Why don't you let me worry about my reputation?"

Lynn gave a bark of laughter. "Because

you obviously won't do it! You came here to help us. I won't be the ruination of your public image."

That won her a chuckle that made her want to kick him in the shin. She tried to pull out of his grasp, but he held her in place with ridiculous ease.

"An hour ago you accused me of using my offer of help as a ruse to get you into my bed!" he exclaimed, blue eyes glittering with humor. "Now you're worried about ruining me?"

She scowled at him. "So I was wrong. So sue me. You're a stand-up guy. Now go home."

"Nope. I'm not letting you stay here alone. You can go back to the other house and I'll keep watch here or you can stay here with me."

"I'll call Lillian," Lynn said, having no intention of following through. The initial burst of fear had long since burned off. She didn't feel endangered, and neither did she feel incapable of staying alone. The rock hurler had made his point and gone home. She doubted he would be back tonight.

"Does Lillian have a husband who can come with her?"

"No. He died four or five years ago."

"Then you can call Lillian and the three of us will stay here together. I'm not leaving women here unprotected."

A sigh slipped from between Lynn's lips as she regarded the man before her. She supposed she could have lied to him and told him Lillian had a husband, but she doubted it would have done her any good. For one thing, she was out of practice. Lies didn't trip that easily from her tongue anymore. For another, the stubborn set of that granite jaw told her Erik wouldn't leave until he was satisfied as to her safety. The idea touched her in a place she hadn't allowed anyone near in a long, long time.

"Oh, for crying out loud," she complained, looking everywhere but at Erik. "All the rotten, unscrupulous politicians in the world and I have to get the one who thinks he's Lancelot."

Erik chuckled to himself. The lady didn't like being thwarted. She was too stubborn and too brave for her own good. Her eyes glittered with suppressed anger. Her soft, pretty mouth turned down in a slight exaggeration of its natural pout. She had the temper of a hellcat. It was a wonder she hadn't jumped out the kitchen window, run the culprit to the ground, and pounded the snot out of him. He had little doubt that she could do it if she really wanted to. Despite her size and the impression of physical fragility, he had the feeling she was one tough little cookie, a sleek little cat who could hold her own in a fight. The trouble was, he wanted to hold it for her, and she didn't like the idea one little bit.

*Well, tough, Ms. Shaw, because you're going to have to put up with me.*

She was too intriguing a package to walk away from. Too pretty, too wary. Her combination of toughness and vulnerability tugged at his heart in a way that was a unique experience for him.

No, he wasn't leaving her alone tonight, or tomorrow, or any day soon.

"Faint heart never won fair lady," he said, gentling his hold on her shoulders as she sighed, apparently resigning herself to her fate.

A sad smile tilted one corner of her mouth. "You don't want to win me, Sir Erik," she said softly, her eyes looking suddenly very old and very weary. "I'm no vestal virgin."

"Did I say I was looking for one?"

No, Lynn thought, but that was what he needed: someone chaste of heart, pure as the driven snow — or at least as pure as

71

the average citizen — someone good and golden to stand beside him on the campaign trail.

"I hear they're highly overrated, those vestal virgins," he murmured, lowering his head. "No spark." He brushed his mouth across hers, making her shiver as the contact sent a rain of stardust along her nerve endings. "No fire," he whispered, repeating the caress.

She should have walked away. She scolded herself for not doing it even as she tipped her head back. She should have moved and maintained a sane, safe distance. But she didn't. She was tired, and an old, too-familiar loneliness was wearing through her armor in big rusty patches. The idea of being held for a moment was too appealing. To feel his masculine warmth envelop her and take her away from reality for just a minute was too tempting. It's just a kiss, she told herself. What harm could there be in one kiss?

He settled his mouth against hers carefully, tenderly, as if he thought she might break. His gentleness was something so rare, so sweet, it brought an ache of tears to her throat. She closed her eyes against the mist that threatened, not wanting Erik to see it or question it.

With the sudden darkness came the sense of falling, floating. She clutched his arms, at biceps so muscled she couldn't begin to close her hands around them. She hung on to him, the only thing solid in a world turned suddenly to pure sensation. He splayed his hands across the small of her back and pulled her close, fusing them together in the maelstrom of passion that had been released.

Lynn trembled at the strength of it, at the strength of her own response. Her body seemed to melt against Erik's, the instinct to seek out his solid warmth overriding the instinct to protect herself. She let her guard drop and simply let the experience sweep her up in the whirlwind, let herself experience every taste, every texture, let her heightened senses soak it all in like a dry sponge.

He tasted warm and sweet, like something she had been craving for a long time without knowing what to call it. She welcomed the gentle invasion of his tongue, sighing softly as he explored her mouth, trembling again at the symbolism. He was invading her body, crossing a line she had let no man cross in a long time. It frightened her and excited her all at once in a confusing swirl of emotions. The tips of her breasts seemed suddenly unbearably sensitive as they pressed against the hard muscles of his chest. At the core of her femininity, a restless sensation stirred and teased, tempting her to press closer to him.

The fear won out in the end. This was happening too fast, when it shouldn't have been happening at all. She had no business letting this man get this close. Lynn couldn't quite believe she had let things go this far. A simple kiss was all it was supposed to be.

Erik felt her tense, sensed her pulling away from him even though she was still in his arms and pressed against the length of him. He raised his head reluctantly, opening his eyes like a man coming out of a trance. Lynn stared up at him, looking as stunned as he felt. He let her ease away from him, too aware of the level of arousal to which this one "simple" kiss had taken them both. He let her back away a step, but hung on to her shoulders, though whether it was to keep her from running or to keep himself from falling over he couldn't have said.

They stared at each other for a long moment, awareness quivering in the air between them. Finally Erik nodded.

"I think I know the perfect chaperon."

"Oh, my, yes," Father Bartholomew said as he burrowed into the folds of his sleeping bag on the couch.

He had shed his clerical uniform for a rumpled gray sweat suit from Holy Cross Seminary. His hair stuck up in odd tufts at the crown of his head, suggesting he had already been in bed when Erik had gone to fetch him. But he had jumped at the chance to keep vigil at the house, scurrying to gather his things together as if he feared the offer might be rescinded before he got his chance at adventure.

He propped himself up now against the arm of the sofa, his face aglow. "This is quite an adventure for me. I feel a little like Father Dowling from the mysteries. You don't suppose we might catch the culprit trying to sneak in?"

Erik started to say no, but the little priest looked so hopeful behind the lenses of his crooked glasses, he didn't have the heart to disappoint him. "It's a possibility."

"Oh, my," Father Bartholomew breathed, eyes round. "I haven't been in on anything this exciting since my mission days in Africa. I was serving with some Jesuit fathers in Kenya. Those Jesuits can be wild men, you know." He chuckled and burrowed deeper into his nest. "Oh, the stories I could tell . . ."

Lynn shot a wry look at Erik, fighting to contain her smile. If nothing else, they were making Father Bartholomew's day. "Thank you again for coming over, Father. I probably would have been fine here alone, but Senator Gunther insisted —"

"Don't think a thing of it, dear!" the priest said, holding up a hand to forestall her explanation. "I'm glad to be of service. A sentry for God. Looking out for mischief makers and hanky-panky." His cheeks colored suddenly and his eyes and mouth made three perfect O's. "Not that I was expecting the two of you — I mean — My, no."

"That's all right, Father," Lynn said, dodging his earnest expression, hoping he couldn't see from her telltale blush that he'd already missed out on the hanky-panky. "Good night."

"Good night, Lynn, dear. Sleep well."

They left the father in the living room as he wiggled down into his sleeping bag like a boy at scout camp. Erik walked beside Lynn to the foot of the stairs in the hall. She had to fight the urge to bolt up the steps in order to escape the warm scrutiny of his eyes. Her senses seemed stuck in high gear, making her too aware of every-thing about him — the way he walked, the subtle scent of his aftershave, the way his watch looked on his wrist, how blond the hair on his arm looked against his tanned skin.

"Well, I don't think we have to worry about bad publicity, do you?" he said, his voice low and threaded with wry amuse-ment. "No one would suspect us of having a wild night of hot, passionate sex while we had a priest for a chaperon."

"No, I guess not." Lynn trudged up two steps, her hand lingering on the newel post. She twisted around toward him hastily. "Not that anything would have happened without him being here," she in-sisted.

Erik rocked back on his heels, his ex-pression mockingly stern, eyes twinkling, lips twitching. "Oh, my, no."

Lynn ground her teeth and scowled at him. "Nothing would have. Nothing will."

A little gasp caught in her throat as he sprang up on the first step. His eyes were level with hers, as blue as the sky on a cloudless fall day. They seemed to catch her in a tractor beam that made it impos-sible to move or look away.

"Something already has," he whispered,

that gentle, knowing smile curling the corners of his lips. "Here's to what comes next."

He brushed a soft, sweet kiss on her cheek and stepped back down. "Good night, Lynn."

"Good night, Senator."

He chuckled at that and sauntered back to the living room. Lynn stood on the stairs and watched him go, her head throbbing at the idea of what might come next.

# — 4 —

Morning came much too soon for Lynn's liking. She awakened with gritty eyes and a head that felt as if it had been stuffed with cotton. Her usual migraine hangover. It hadn't helped that she'd gotten precious little sleep, or that what sleep she'd gotten had been plagued with visions of Erik Gunther. She'd spent most of the night lying on the mattress on the floor of what would be one of the resident rooms, staring at the ceiling and trying to will herself not to dream about that kiss. But even now, as she cracked open her eyelids and squinted against the morning light pouring in through the window, she could still feel Erik Gunther's body against her, still feel his enveloping warmth and strength, still taste his mouth on hers.

Grumbling, she pushed herself into a sitting position and raked her hair back out of her eyes. According to her watch it was nearly seven and, while she would have liked nothing better than to crawl back under the blanket and sleep for another day or two — or better yet, magically transport herself to her own bed in her apartment across town and sleep for another day or two — there was a long day and a lot of work ahead. The girls would be living in this house by nightfall. How long they would be able to stay here was anyone's guess, but they would definitely be sleeping here tonight.

How would the girls react to the hostility in this neighborhood? Lynn wondered as she padded barefoot across the hardwood floor in search of her overnight bag. Her jeans lay where she'd stepped out of them the night before. She hadn't had the energy to do more than that, and had slept in her panties and T-shirt. She dug a fresh T-shirt from her suitcase and changed with a minimum of fuss, her mind on her girls.

There were currently five residents, ranging in age from fourteen to seventeen. Barbara Wheeler and Michelle Jenner were from Rochester, both from dysfunctional, single-parent families, both fresh from a substance-abuse rehab program at St. Mary's Hospital. The other three girls — Regan Mitchell, Tracy Brogan, and Christine Rickman — were from other parts of the state. Christine was fifteen and pregnant. Tracy had a history as a runaway and a background with an abusive father.

Regan was the newest challenge. It was Regan who worried Lynn the most.

From the outside Regan Mitchell appeared to have everything going for her. She was from a "good" family. Her father had an important position at Honeywell in Minneapolis. The family lived in the affluent suburb of Minnetonka. Regan had been given every advantage. What she hadn't been given was love. Her father was a cold, demanding man, her mother caught up in charity work and social life. The Mitchells had more or less expected their children to raise themselves, to automatically grow up to be perfect and productive and responsible. But that hadn't happened with Regan. She had grown up feeling empty and unloved, and she had filled that emptiness with anger, bitterness, resentment, rebellion.

She had been in and out of trouble for the last three years, and at sixteen was in danger of being declared a lost cause. She had run away, dabbled in drugs, shoplifted at every major department store in the metro area. Her friends had been a familiar crowd at juvenile hall. Regan herself presented a tough I-don't-give-a-damn facade, but Lynn was convinced it was just that — a facade to hide the vulnerable, lonely girl who was so desperately in need of a real friend.

Regan would be the most sensitive to Elliot Graham's brand of disapproval. She had trouble fitting in, resisted fitting in, daring people to like her in spite of her terrible attitude. To date, few people had cared enough to go through the hassle. She had made the rounds of the "better" juvenile homes in the Twin Cities, and had finally been shipped down to Horizon House. Now Horizon House itself was being shuffled around, rejected, and disapproved of. Lynn doubted the situation would do anything to help Regan settle in.

She stepped into a clean pair of worn-out jeans, pulled on her battered canvas sneakers without undoing the laces, and yanked open the bedroom door, determined to face the day, ready or not. Sitting on the floor just outside the room was a plate with a fortune cookie on it. The cookie had been cracked open and the end of a strip of white paper stuck out of the shell, beckoning the curious to look and see what the future might hold in store.

Lynn scowled at it, stepped around it, took a backward step toward the bathroom, eyeing the cookie as if it were bait in a trap. She told herself she didn't care what it said. She wasn't some sap ready and willing to believe an arbitrary sentence stuffed into a cookie at a factory a thousand miles away. Still, she hesitated. Her gaze darted up and down the hall. The coast was clear. Cursing her own curiosity, she bent and snatched the message out of the shell.

"Good things are coming to you in the due course of time," she read aloud. Giving a snort of disbelief, she stuffed the note into her pocket and headed down the hall to try to restore some order to her hair.

The sound of Father Bartholomew's voice led the way to the kitchen.

"Shredded bran, oat bran, bran nuts, that's all the woman will buy. I tell you, my breakfast bowl usually looks like something you should feed to a workhorse. Bless her heart, I know Mrs. Ingram means well, but all that bran can put a real dent in a man's morning, if you know what I mean. I try to tell her. Why, just the other day I said to her, 'Agnes, when I preach that we should purge ourselves, I mean it in a spiritual sense!' "

Warm, husky laughter rolled out of the kitchen, stopping Lynn in her tracks just outside the door. She had been half hoping Senator Gunther would have been off to some essential breakfast meeting with his staff or teeing off with some grand poohbah. No such luck.

He was sitting at the far end of the kitchen table, looking very much at home in his rumpled white polo shirt. His golden-blond hair looked finger-combed, slightly tousled, much too sexy. The hair, combined with the morning beard that shadowed the strong planes of his cheeks, made him look like a rock star, some teen idol just waiting for a herd of adoring young girls to hurl themselves at him. He sat with his elbows on the table, big shoulders hunched, a steaming cup of coffee in front of him and a Twinkie in his hand.

The Twinkie got her. She could have steeled herself against the screen-star looks and the man's-man aura, but how could she fight against a Twinkie? How could she maintain her cool against a white knight with a weakness for junk food?

"Oh, dear! Good morning, Lynn!" Father Bartholomew twisted around in his seat to give her a bright smile. As usual, his glasses were askew. He had obviously made an effort to glue his hair into submission with something that smelled like motor oil, but one recalcitrant section still stood up in a little fan of spikes at the crown of his head. "I didn't hear you come down."

"Good morning, Father." She nodded in Erik's direction but avoided looking right at him, keeping her eyes on his half-eaten Twinkie. "Senator."

"Senator Gunther went out and got us some treats for breakfast."

"I see that. Twinkies. This is my lucky day." Lynn made a beeline to the coffee maker and filled an empty mug.

"I'd put them on my grocery list," the father said, "but Mrs. Ingram wouldn't buy them. She's worried about my cholesterol and fat intake. I'd go out and get some for myself, but I don't do well in these big supermarkets. I don't have a very good sense of direction, I'm afraid."

"For letting us use this house, Father, I will gladly keep you supplied with Twinkies," Lynn said, leaning back against the counter.

"Horizon House is a worthy cause, dear," he declared, a rare gleam of stubbornness coming into his dark little eyes. "I won't let anyone tell me different."

Lynn thought the bishop might have something to say on the subject after he met with Elliot Graham, but she held her

85

tongue. It was too early in the day to be contentious. There was no point in it anyway. She would only upset Father Bartholomew, and that was the last thing she wanted to do. He was such a sweet, dear man. The only person who'd been willing to step forward and help them — until Erik Gunther.

"I'd better be going," the priest said, pushing his chair back from the table. He rose and reached for the Twinkies, stuffing three into the pouch on his sleep-wrinkled sweatshirt. "If I don't get to morning mass before the ladies finish the rosary, I'll be in the doghouse, I can tell you. I'll stop by later to see how things are going."

Lynn bid him good-bye and watched with a sinking heart as he let himself out the back door and scuttled across the yard, headed for the rectory. Their chaperon was gone. Almost instantly the level of sexual tension thickened in the air like a sudden fog.

"How's the headache?" Erik asked.

"Gone thanks," she murmured, burying her nose in the steam from her coffee cup.

It wasn't quite the truth. There was still a kernel of pain lodged above her right eye like a glowing ember waiting for fuel so it could burst into flame again. It might stay there for days, haunting her with the possibility of another full-fledged migraine, but she had no desire to share that information with Erik.

She could feel that incredibly magnetic blue gaze on her, searching, assessing. She just barely resisted the urge to check her hair. This was not good. She didn't have time to be worrying about her appearance, wondering if he would think she was a slob because he'd only ever seen her in holey jeans and college T-shirts. That was her usual uniform, because it was comfortable and unthreatening to her girls. What did she care if Senator Gunther thought she was underdressed?

"The coffee is decaf," he said. "People who suffer from migraines should avoid caffeine. I was just reading up on it this morning in *Newsweek*."

Lynn wrinkled her nose at the coffee and his concern. She didn't want him reading up on migraines or making her special coffee, even if it did seem like an awfully sweet thing for him to do. The kiss had been a mistake, a moment of weakness. Now, in the bright light of day, she could see it for what it was: sheer foolishness. She couldn't have a relationship with Erik Gunther. There was no point in pursuing something that could only end in disappointment.

"Have a seat," he invited, gesturing magnanimously toward the chair to his right.

She gave the chair a suspicious look, wrapped her hands around her coffee mug, and held it against her chest. "I'll stand, thanks."

A muscle in Erik's jaw tightened. "You know," he said with a bright, square smile, "I think I'll stand too. I like standing. I don't get to do enough standing in my day-to-day life."

He pushed his chair back from the table and rose, Twinkie in hand. He kept his gaze on Lynn, letting her know he wouldn't be so easily daunted. She was trying to put distance between them, physically and emotionally, trying to ease the effect of the kiss they had shared. He had no intention of letting her get away with it. He was a grown man with his share of experience, but he'd never felt anything like what he'd felt in that kiss. If she thought he would blithely walk away from that, she had another think coming.

She scowled at him as he took up a stance beside her, leaning casually back against the counter, ankles crossed, coffee cup in one hand, Twinkie in the other. He half expected her to scoot over to the table and sit down, but she held her ground. Stubborn. Erik fought a smile. He couldn't remember ever finding stubbornness an attractive trait in a woman. With Lynn it was all but turning him on. He wanted to turn and corral her against the counter as he had the night before and give her a good-morning kiss that would have her thinking about going back to bed — and taking him with her.

He was falling like a rock. He'd known her all of twelve hours and he was feeling as besotted as a teenager. Instead of being disgusted with himself, Erik wanted to laugh. He'd waited a long time to feel this way. It felt pretty good, even though the lady in question was reluctant. He had faith in his ability to win her over. If there was one thing his father had taught him before his death, it was that if he set his mind to it and worked hard enough he could have anything he wanted.

He wanted Lynn Shaw. No question about that, he thought, letting his gaze drift down from her thick, unruly mane, over the delicate features of her face to the small, proud breasts that gave a delightful dimension to her gray Purdue T-shirt. For just a second he indulged himself in the fantasy of lifting the hem of that T-shirt and giving his full attention to those breasts — stroking, teasing, tasting . . .

"Did you get your fortune cookie?" He glanced at her sideways and took a bite out of his breakfast, forcing the fantasy and the heat it had generated from his mind.

Lynn squeezed her hands around her coffee mug as she watched him lick a fleck of cream filling from the corner of his mouth and cursed herself inwardly as her nipples tightened and tingled. "Oh, yes," she replied in a dry tone. "I must be in store for something. Why, just last week I got a letter from Ed McMahon telling me I might have won ten million dollars. Now this. It's too weird."

"You don't believe in fate?"

She thought about that for a long moment, staring across the room at the dented refrigerator. She had seen too many ruined lives, too many heartbreaks. If there was such a creature as fate, it had an exceedingly wide sadistic streak. It was less painful to think that life just happened. Some people screwed up and some people didn't. Some people grew up to be Erik Gunthers and some led lives like she had led.

"No," she whispered. "I don't."

"I do. I might never have met you if Horizon House hadn't lost its lease. I'd call that fate."

Lynn gave a derisive little sniff. "I call it a pain in the butt. You've obviously never had to move a houseful of teenage girls plus the accumulated junk from three offices."

"Pessimist," he accused with a good-natured chuckle.

She tipped her head, wincing a little at the sudden nip of pain above her eye. "That's me."

"Yeah, and you're a fibber too," Erik said, turning toward her. He leaned a hip against the counter and stared down at her, his eyes narrowed in speculation and concern. "You've still got that headache. I can see it in your eyes."

He set his cup aside, popped the last of his Twinkie in his mouth, and wiped his fingers on his shirt. Lynn tried to sidle away as he reached for her, but he caught her with a firm yet gentle hand, turning to trap her between himself and the counter.

"Be still," he ordered, tawny brows pulling together in consternation. "You're like a wild horse, shying away from me every time I try to touch you."

"Did it ever occur to you that I don't

want to be touched?" she snapped, moving her head from side to side, trying to dodge his hand.

"No," he said bluntly. "It occurred to me that you're afraid to have me touch you."

Fire flared in her emerald eyes. Her chin came up a notch. "I am not."

"Liar."

He spread his fingers into her hair and settled them against her scalp, rubbing gently. "Relax," he ordered. "And close your eyes, too, while you're at it. Go on."

Lynn squeezed her eyes shut, determined to hold herself rigid in his grasp. She wouldn't give in to him. No doubt everyone gave in to him — Erik the Great, destined for big things. It was time he didn't get his way. He needed to see he couldn't win her over with a smile and a magic touch. . . .

But, dammit, it felt wonderful. He had found a spot with his middle finger that made her want to groan aloud, and when he brought his thumb against her forehead to rub at the knot of tension there, she did groan aloud, a soft soughing sound that slipped between her lips without her permission. Muscles loosened of their own volition and she relaxed, melting against the counter.

"That feels good, doesn't it?" Erik whispered.

"Yes," she admitted grudgingly.

Erik chuckled. "Why do I think you'd rather have gotten a migraine than proved me right?"

Lynn let her eyelids drift up to half-mast and looked up at him through the barrier of her lashes. His expression was soft, amused, sweet. Why couldn't he have been pompous and arrogant? She regularly cut off pompous, arrogant men at the knees and sent them crawling home. But this one . . . this one was dangerous.

"I'm not here to hurt you, Lynn," he murmured, the sincerity in his eyes almost enough to bring a lump to her throat.

"No," she said, scrambling inwardly for a defense. "You're here on a mission of mutual benefit."

Irritation flashed in his eyes like lightning. His hand stilled, then slipped away from her and settled on his hip. "I thought we settled this point last night. I'm here because I want to help."

"Why?" Lynn challenged, setting her coffee cup aside. "Yes, it's a worthy cause, but Horizon was a worthy cause a year ago when the landlord was raising our rent and refusing to make repairs on the house, and we never saw you then. Admit it, Senator, you wouldn't be here now if someone hadn't deemed this situation not only worthy but *news*worthy."

"I'm not the one who called the TV crew last night."

"But you're the one who got the publicity."

"What difference does it make?" Erik shook his head and reined in his temper. He had a feeling she was deliberately provoking him, picking a fight to put more distance between them.

"This argument is pointless," he said, sliding his hand back into her hair and renewing the massage. He inched a little closer, casually bracing his free hand on the counter beside Lynn's hip. "You know what I do about pointless arguments?" He smiled as he bent his head toward hers. "I end them."

It was the perfect opportunity for Lynn to draw a line and push him back across it. She should have. But she didn't. She silently cursed her sudden immobility as Erik's mouth descended on hers. As if she had suddenly lost control of her motor skills, she simply stood there and let him kiss her. And worse, she let herself absorb the sensations and enjoy them.

His lips were both firm and soft, warm and satiny. He tasted like coffee and sweetness. His morning beard rasped gently against her cheek as he tilted his head to deepen the kiss. With the tip of his tongue he traced the shape of her lips, then gently asked for permission to slip inside. And while Lynn didn't exactly grant it, she didn't exactly deny it either.

Erik interpreted her nonresponse in his favor, taking what he wanted, easing his tongue into her mouth. He liked the taste of morning on her — coffee and toothpaste. She tasted fresh, as if he were the first man to experience her. The idea brought a rush of possessiveness and the primitive heat of the male need to claim her as his. He stroked his left hand through her thick, soft hair to cup the back of her head and hold her at the angle he liked best. His right hand migrated from the counter to the gentle curve of her hip, fingers kneading, pulling her closer. Her hands came up against his chest, as if she meant to push him away, but the action never came.

He kissed her as if they had all the time in the world, taking full advantage of the fact that she wasn't fighting him. He could sense her hesitancy, but it was being overridden for the moment by something stronger. The spark that had ignited between them the night before was struggling to come to life, and Erik was determined to do all he could to fan it into a flame.

Still, when Lynn finally tried to end the kiss, he let her. Some scrap of common sense that hadn't been completely blown away by touching her told him not to push too many boundaries too soon. She was wary of him. If he let her keep too much distance between them, they would never get the chance to explore this passion blooming between them. But if he allowed himself to be too aggressive, he would ruin his chances altogether.

"See?" he whispered, his head still bent near hers, his gaze searching her eyes for her reaction. "Argument's over."

Lynn swallowed a breath. A belated tremor shivered down her from the crown of her head to the tips of her toes. "You make a very convincing closing statement, Senator," she said breathlessly.

"Erik," he commanded gently.

"E-Erik."

He smiled at that. His name stumbled out of her mouth like a word from a foreign language. He stroked his hand over her hair and started to draw her close again, just wanting to hold her for a minute longer.

"Care to make a rebuttal, Counselor Shaw?"

Lynn started to shake her head. "I don't think —"

"No. Your trouble is, you think *too* much."

That was hardly the case, Lynn wanted to tell him. All her life she had gotten into trouble for acting, not thinking. She ran on emotion and instinct, action and reaction. Her emotionalism was what had set her apart in her family. Her father had been a man of logic. Her sister, Rebecca, had been the same way — pragmatic, analytical, reserved. And their staid, controlled personalities had only provoked Lynn to behave in an even more outrageously emotional way. Even now, with her rebellion behind her, she tended to act first. Her altercation with Elliot Graham the night before had been a perfect example.

Martha's voice came bellowing down the hall and snapped Lynn from her trance. Her hands were still pressed flat against Erik's chest and she gave him a shove, intending to bolt away from him. He gave her that infuriating little smile of his, holding her a second longer, then releasing her. The kitchen door swung open and Martha barged in, arms laden with grocery bags. She was followed by three teenage girls, each with a bulging bag in their arms. The bags went on the table. The eyes went to Erik Gunther. Tracy, Michelle, and Barbara stared at him, bug-eyed and slack-jawed, as if they'd never seen a live man before.

"Hunk-o-rama!" Michelle breathed, nudging Barbara with a bony elbow.

Tracy Brogan leaned toward the others, dark eyes stuck on Erik. "Do you think he comes with the house?" she whispered.

Erik blushed and tried to muster a stern look that had no effect whatsoever on the girls. They studied him with open curiosity as they stood there in a tight little knot. Teenage girls. Even as a teenager himself, he hadn't been able to figure them out. They were like an alien life-form to him. And they looked it, too, he thought as he took in the overpermed hairdo with bangs spritzed into frozen fountains of hair springing high up from their foreheads. He was a man who regularly argued important issues with the most powerful men in the state, but he was suddenly way out of his element and he knew it.

Lynn cleared her throat loudly in an effort to gain their attention. "Girls," she said. "This is State Senator Gunther. Senator, Tracy Brogan, Michelle Jenner, and Barbara Wheeler."

Erik nodded politely. He was suddenly aware of the state of his appearance — the rumpled polo shirt with the tails hanging out, chinos that were in dire need of a steam iron, a day's growth of beard on his face. He didn't look like a state senator. He looked as if he'd spent the night, and the bright gleam in the girls' eyes told him they thought so too.

"We had a little trouble here last night after you and Lillian left, Martha," he said, feeling the need to connect with an adult. "Father Bartholomew and I bunked in the living room. We didn't think Lynn should stay here alone."

"Trouble?" Martha's fleshy face folded into a look of concern as she pulled a gallon of milk out of a grocery bag and turned toward the refrigerator. "Land o' Goshen! What happened to the refrigerator?"

Lynn rubbed a hand across her mouth, half-glad for the dent in the appliance. It would keep Martha's shrewd eyes from catching the fact that she looked thoroughly kissed. "Um, it's a long story. Can we wait until everyone's here to go over it?"

Martha ignored the question. She thrust the milk at Tracy and took Lynn by the shoulders. "Are you all right?"

"I'm fine. Really." Lynn met her employer's gaze without flinching, putting on a poker face that would have won her a bundle in Vegas. It didn't fool Martha. Her gaze slid meaningfully to Erik and back, and a ghost of a smile claimed her bright red lips.

The kitchen door swung open again and Lillian strode in, looking her usual prim self. Her face was set in stern lines of disapproval, and Lynn could tell by her long, slow deep breath that her patience was nearing an end. The reason for Lillian's mood stepped into the kitchen behind her — five feet eight inches of pretty, dark-haired, blue-eyed trouble.

"God, this place is a dump," Regan Mitchell pronounced, her voice dripping disdain. She gave the kitchen a cursory, narrow-eyed look and crossed her arms over the front of her black tank top as her gaze sliced across the room to Lynn. "It doesn't even have cable."

Lynn shrugged. "Believe it or not, most of the great people in the history of the world managed to grow up without MTV."

"Not that you'd be watching it if we did have it," Lillian intoned imperiously.

Regan gave a huff of disgust. Lynn looked to Martha for an explanation.

"While you were busy here defacing the kitchen appliances, we were having a little crisis of our own. Regan went out for a while last night without notifying anyone."

The girl rolled her eyes and sighed the sigh of the teenaged oppressed. "So I went downtown. Big deal. There wasn't anything else to do. This place is so boring I can't stand it."

"Yeah, well we can't stand *you,* either," Tracy Brogan sneered, giving her fellow resident a malevolent look.

"Tracy, that's enough," Lynn admonished quietly. "Lillian, why don't you take Tracy and Michelle and Barbara upstairs and try to decide how the bedrooms should be arranged."

The group marched out, Lillian with her regal nose raised, Tracy bumping shoulders with Regan on her way past, Barbara and Michelle still casting looks of amazement at Erik. Martha started putting groceries away, her manner relaxed.

Lynn went to the table and plucked a Twinkie off the plate, her attention gradually drifting back to Regan, who still stood braced for battle. Her mouth was painted a hideous shade of dark plum and set in a grim pout. Defiance radiated from her like an aura — defiance of authority, defiance of anyone trying to get close. She even defied her own budding beauty. She had hacked her hair into a ragged style that looked as if rats had chewed it off as she slept. She dressed in the look Lynn called "The Grim Reaper Goes G.I." — anything black and unflattering on milky-white skin, and combat boots. A safety pin and a cross hung from one ear. A tiny ruby studded one nostril. It was a look calculated to make her seem ugly and unapproachable. Lynn knew; she had worn her own version of it for a time.

"Want a Twinkie?" she asked, holding up the yellow cake. The question won her nothing more than a derisive snort. "So where'd you go last night?"

"Nowhere."

"That must have been exciting."

"I went to Peace Plaza to hang out, okay? Big freaking deal."

From the corner of her eye, Lynn caught Erik's scowl as he helped Martha unpack grocery bags. She looked back at Regan in time to catch the girl examining a nasty scrape on the knuckles of her right hand.

"Are you okay?"

"I'm fine. Like you really care."

"I do really care."

"Because my parents are paying you to."

"No, but I'm sure you'd rather think that, so I'm not going to argue with you. What happened?"

Regan's gaze flicked away. "I tripped on the sidewalk."

She wasn't a very convincing liar. Lynn hadn't figured out yet if her ineptitude at prevarication was intentional or natural. She suspected it was a little of both. She let the subject drop for the moment. She didn't like the idea of Regan wandering the streets at night, and neither did she like the idea that something had happened to cause that abrasion, but probing deeper now would only win her more defiance. She took a bite of Twinkie and changed tack.

"Regan, I know you have a problem with rules," she said calmly, dipping a finger into the cream filling, "but we really need you to follow them right now. Things are getting pretty touchy with this move."

"What the hell do I care?" the girl snapped. "I hate this freaking place. I wouldn't care if someone burned it to the freaking ground."

"Hey!" Erik barked, wheeling around from the cupboard with a thunderous expression on his face. "I've heard about enough of your mouth."

Regan's chin lifted. "So why don't you freaking leave?"

Lynn watched as Erik's face turned red clear to the tips of his ears. The muscles in his jaw tightened, his nostrils flared. Seeing his temper escalate reminded her of her father. A little part of her heart sank. She had already guessed he wouldn't be the tolerant sort, but some small corner of her heart had been holding out hope. Foolish heart. He was an authoritarian, a man who lived by the rules, a straight arrow. He wouldn't understand girls like Regan. He said he was here because he cared, but his caring didn't extend beyond the issue itself.

She abandoned the Twinkie and moved away from the table just as Erik advanced on Regan with a finger raised in warning.

"Miss Shaw is trying to help you. The least you can do is be civil to her."

Regan's eyes snapped with rebellion. "Who the hell are you to tell me what to do?"

Lynn intervened with graceful diplomacy, putting herself between them. "Regan, this is Senator Gunther."

"Whoopee-do."

Erik sucked in a breath as he turned a darker shade of maroon. Lynn shot him a pointed look. "The senator was just leaving," she said sharply, warding off whatever tirade he had been about to embark on.

Erik started to refute her statement, but the ominous glitter in her eyes made him bite his tongue. He backed away a step as Lynn turned toward her young charge, ushering her through the door.

"Let's go put something on that scrape, then you can help Martha get the kitchen in order."

"Maybe I don't want to help Martha."

"Tough spit. That's your job."

Erik sat on the front step of the house, staring glumly at the street. It was a warm, cloudy day. Down the block a group of little girls were playing a game that involved a lot of high-pitched squealing. Next door St. Stephen's loomed like a small medieval castle cut from honey-colored limestone. On the sidewalk in front of the church an elderly woman made her way along with a walker. This was a quiet neighborhood. There seemed to be little traffic, pedestrian or otherwise. He looked across the street at the tree-shaded house that was Elliot Graham's home and wondered if Graham had had Regan Mitchell specifically in mind when he'd said Erik should meet the girls of Horizon House before making a judgment.

She had certainly punched his button, Erik admitted with a rueful sigh. And his reaction to her had punched one of Lynn's. He'd felt every defensive shield she had go up as she'd stood between him and Regan, and whatever ground he'd gained with her up to that second had been yanked right from under his feet.

The screen door swung open behind him and Lynn stepped out. He looked at her over his shoulder, noting the way she held her arms crossed tightly against herself and the way her lush, pretty mouth turned down at the corners, and his heart sank a little lower. The lady was steamed.

"I'll try to keep Regan out of earshot when you're doing your next little publicity appearance on behalf of our cause," she said sardonically.

"I'm sorry I lost my temper," Erik said, pushing himself to his feet and turning to face her. "I didn't like the way she was talking to you."

One winged black brow lifted in imperious question. "Really? And how did you think she would talk to me? She's hurt and angry and bitter. Her parents have abandoned her, emotionally and physically. You'd probably love them. They're very politically correct people. Their answer to every problem is to throw money at it."

"Oh, give me a break," Erik said irritably. He was angry with himself for losing his temper, but he was equally angry with Regan for provoking him and with Lynn for putting up with the girl's attitude and foul mouth. "What am I supposed to say here? Poor little Regan, her rich parents don't pay enough attention to her? That gives her the right to act any way she wants? I don't think so. I had it a lot tougher than her when I was a kid and I didn't go around mouthing off to adults and running around doing God knows what all night."

"Well, good for you, Erik," Lynn snapped. "That makes you better and bigger and stronger than the rest of us. You had a hard life and you came out shining like a champion. Maybe we should make you king of the world."

He heaved a sigh and rubbed a hand across the stubble on his jaw. This was working out just swell. He needed a shower and a shave and a chance to regroup mentally. "Look, maybe I was out of line —"

"There's no 'maybe' about it. My girls answer to me, Senator, not you. They don't need you to hold up your high standards of conduct as something to measure themselves against, and they don't need your disapproval."

Erik held his hands up in surrender. "I said I was sorry. I just have a little problem sympathizing with kids who have advantages and still turn out like Regan. Let's not get into a big fight about it."

Lynn clamped her mouth into a tight line and glared at him. He stepped up onto the porch, taking away her height advantage. Hoping to take the edge off her defensiveness as well, he settled his big hands on her shoulders.

"We're on the same side, remember?" he said softly, giving her his most apologetic smile as he shuffled a little closer. "Partners. Friends." He lowered his head, meaning to give her a little kiss, but she shrugged off his touch and stepped back.

"My father was a professor at Notre Dame," she said, her voice tight and husky

108

with some emotion she wouldn't let show. "I made Regan look like an honor student. Advantages aren't everything."

Hands on his hips, Erik hung his head and gave another long, defeated sigh. "I really stuck my foot in it, didn't I?"

"Right up to your ankle."

"You know, I wasn't very good at being a teenager," he said candidly. "I think I have a few things to learn. Maybe you could teach me?"

It was more a ploy to spend time with her than a plea for help. Erik's conscience nipped him, but for once he ignored it. He wanted to know more about Lynn Shaw. If he had to take a crash course in juvenile delinquents to get what he wanted, then so be it.

Lynn's eyes narrowed as she took another step back from him. She tightened her arms against her chest and shook her head. She'd made the mistake of letting him get too close too many times already. Getting involved with him would be an absolute disaster. She wouldn't change his mind about girls like Regan — girls like she had been. He was too firmly indoctrinated in midwestern moral righteousness, the Scandinavian-Lutheran ethics of proper behavior. He probably had more in common with Elliot Graham than he did with her. He had it in his head now that he wanted her, but in the end he would disapprove of her the same way he disapproved of Regan, and she would end up standing alone with the pieces of another broken relationship crumbling in her hands.

"You came here to lend your support to our cause and to get your face in the paper, Senator," she said quietly as she turned toward the door. "Let's just leave it at that."

# — 5 —

"Congratulations, you're page one in the *Post Bulletin* today. Page three in the *Star Tribune* and *Pioneer Press*."

Erik wedged the receiver between his shoulder and ear, frowning as he tightened the knot in the dark green towel he'd hurriedly slung around his hips. His aide went on with all the enthusiasm of a hungry young political hound.

"They called this morning to confirm some facts about your voting record. Lori and I conducted a little impromptu poll afterward and the general feeling so far is that you're a hero for saving women from being thrown into the street. There's been some negative vibes about the delinquent girls, but I think we can downplay that angle and still get you good coverage. What do you think? Erik? Are you still there?"

Erik stood staring out his bedroom window at the lush green woods beyond his backyard. Rob William's words had hit him like a hammer. This was exactly the call he would have expected from his right-hand man. This was the kind of strategy they discussed every day. He'd never given it a second thought. This was the way the game was played. His was a high-profile profession, a profession that hung on public support. Most days he took it in stride. Today his stride faltered as a vision of Lynn's face loomed up in his mind's eye, her expression cynical and accusatory.

"Erik?"

"Yeah, Rob, I'm here," he mumbled. Phone dangling from the fingertips of his left hand, he slowly paced the length of his bed, his bare feet brushing silently across the thick beige carpet. He listened with one ear as his aide filled him in on Elliot Graham's designs on a recently vacated city council seat, then went on to other matters of concern on the agenda.

". . . and we could schedule a press conference if you want, but don't forget you've got lunch with Gary Pressman from *Minnesota Monthly* and a golf date with the governor at three."

"Cancel it."

The voice on the other end of the line was stuck between a chuckle of disbelief and the silence of outright shock. "W-What?"

"You heard me," Erik said decisively. "I can't make it to the Cities today. If

Pressman wants a story, he'll have to come and get it. As for the governor, I think he'll understand if you tell him I had more important things to do than commiserate with him about his slice."

"But — but —"

"Thanks for the info on Graham. I'll touch base later."

They said their good-byes, Rob sounding less than sure about his boss's sudden change of plans. Erik set the phone down on the oak stand beside his bed and went into the bathroom to shave. He went about the task quietly, methodically, his actions automatic, his mind on Lynn.

"You're a jerk," he said to himself at last.

He stood before the sink, half his face lathered with shaving cream. His reflection stared back at him from the mirror, the white beard of foam making him look as if he was in disguise, but he couldn't hide from the scrutiny of his own blue eyes. He'd done exactly what Lynn had accused him of from the first. He had gone to Horizon House concerned with only what was on the surface. They were having trouble with their housing. He would sweep in like the proverbial white knight, save them, and ride on, with the cheers of the grateful echoing behind him. But Horizon's problems went deeper than housing.

He hadn't given much thought to the residents of the house before he'd gone there. He had simply taken up the banner for right, the defense of the defenseless, carelessly believing that that was enough. And once he'd met the girls he'd reacted in a way that put him just a scant notch or two above Elliot Graham on the international scale of cretins. What a hypocrite. He'd fashioned himself as a champion of the oppressed and then looked down his nose at them just as everyone else did. Erik couldn't remember the last time he'd been so ashamed of himself.

*I made Regan look like an honor student.* Lynn's words rang in his ears and he leaned against the marble countertop and groaned at his own stupidity. By disapproving of Regan he had condemned Lynn as well. *You don't want to win me, Sir Erik. I'm no vestal virgin.*

"Aw, Lynn," he whispered, shaking his head. He'd hurt her. They hadn't known each other a full day and already he'd hurt her. He gave his reflection a look of disgust. "Some white knight you are."

The only thing he could do was start over, he thought as he brought his razor up and plied it carefully to the plane of his cheek. He would just have to go back to Horizon House and prove to himself and Lynn Shaw that he could care.

"I just love working with an audience," Lynn said dryly as she hefted a box down from the stack in the back of the rented moving van. She handed it to Martha, who handed it to Tracy. The girl trudged off toward the house with a stormy look on her face, dodging the protestors who paraded up and down the sidewalk, signs bobbing.

Lynn watched them, taking a moment to get her breath in the stifling heat. A very organized bunch, these demonstrators. It seemed they had a schedule. This was the afternoon shift, comprised mostly of people Martha's age, with a few young mothers thrown in for balance. They had come up with a chant, which droned on and on in a bland midwestern monotone: "Save our family neighborhood. Runaways go home. Save our family neighborhood. Runaways go home."

Martha scowled at them. "I'll bet they were a grubby bunch of peasants in a former life," she said as Lynn handed down another box. "Probably the same horde from the Salem witch hunt."

"Well, we're safe for the moment," Lynn

said, her resentment evident in the sarcasm that crackled in her voice. She wiped the sweat from her forehead, brushing her damp bangs out of her eyes. "I'm sure there must be a city ordinance against burning infidels in public. That kind of thing is bad for the image of Camelot."

"So are we," Martha reminded her. She passed her box to Barbara, watching protectively as the girl ducked through the line of demonstrators and all but ran for the house. Shaking her head in disgust, Martha turned and rested her forearms on the bed of the truck. "Speaking of Camelot, I wonder what became of our knight?"

"Oh, I imagine he's gone home to spiff himself up for his next photo opportunity."

Martha absorbed the jibe, her gaze steady and speculative. Lynn could feel it on her, soaking up her expression, her manner, her tension. She turned away on the pretense of looking for a particular box in the jumbled mess in the moving van.

"You were a little hard on him this morning," Martha commented. "Considering he's our only real help so far."

"Father Bartholomew is our only real help so far. All Erik Gunther has done is get himself in the news."

"Oh, I don't think that's *all* he's done."

Lynn jerked around to glare at her friend, using anger and defensiveness as a shield to keep Martha from seeing whatever else might have been there. "What's that supposed to mean?"

"I don't think you should condemn him for losing his temper with Regan," Martha said, ignoring the question. "She would try the patience of the proverbial saint, you know. She had Lillian on the verge of a cerebral hemorrhage this morning. That girl has a positive genius for infuriating people."

"It wasn't just Regan," Lynn charged, digging up every scrap of evidence she had against Erik Gunther to ward off the memory of his kisses. "He was showing his true colors. I told you he wasn't interested in anything more than what this issue could do for his career, and he proved it. Men like Erik Gunther are all style and no substance."

Martha rolled her eyes. "He sure looks substantial to me. The man is a hunk and a half."

"Handsome is as handsome does," Lynn said primly, reaching for another box.

"I'd say handsome did a pretty good job of ruffling your feathers."

"He did not. This whole mess has done the ruffling."

"Really?" Martha arched a brow as she accepted the box of books, then set it aside. "Well, while we're spouting old maxims, maybe you should try this one on for size — 'To thine own self be true.' "

Lynn's retort died on her lips as a motorcade rounded the corner onto their block. She straightened slowly, one hand pressing against the sore spot in her lower back. Erik Gunther's burgundy Thunderbird led the parade, followed by two pickups loaded with people. They pulled over to the curb behind the moving van and the passengers climbed out, looking bright-eyed and ready for action. Dressed in jeans, shorts, and T-shirts, they didn't bear any resemblance to a news crew or any other group that might trail around after a popular politician. A mixture of men and women of various ages, some came armed with cleaning paraphernalia. One man was carrying a cooler. Some of the women held casseroles and cake pans.

Erik himself had shed any semblance of his professional image. A pair of age-faded jeans clung to his lean hips and muscular thighs. The T-shirt he wore was a shade of blue that enhanced his tan and brought out the startling color of his eyes. Stretched across his chest in black ink was an outline of the Mayo Clinic and the line ROCHESTER, MINNESOTA: PREFERRED BY NINE OUT OF TEN SICK PEOPLE. Taking in the total picture, from his tousled blond hair to his sneakers, no one would have guessed he spent most of his life in committee meetings. He looked like a walking ad for healthy outdoor life and hard physical work.

His eyes locked on Lynn's as he came toward the van. Lynn fought the urge to glance around in search of an escape route. She could handle Senator Gunther. Bad choice of words, she groaned inwardly as an image of the two of them entwined in a kiss floated up in her mind's eye.

"I thought you ladies could probably use some help unloading," he said. "So I went out and rounded some up. I called a couple of groups here in town and they were more than willing to send a few volunteers."

In exchange for a favor or two, Lynn thought. Before this was over he would have half the special-interest groups in Rochester in his debt.

"Erik, you're a godsend," Martha declared, patting his arm as he took up a

119

stance beside her at the back of the truck. "At my age I don't even want to move my own body half the time, let along a truck-load of junk."

"Why don't you take a break?" he suggested. "Put your feet up, have some lemonade. Bill there has a coolerful."

"Sounds like a plan to me."

"Lynn, you can go, too, if you like."

"Thanks for giving me your permission, Senator," Lynn said sardonically. "But I'm fine right here."

Martha snorted and headed toward the house, the stream of demonstrators parting for her like the Red Sea. The cleaning crew and kitchen detail trailed after her. The rest of the volunteers hung back by Erik's car, awaiting instructions.

"Suit yourself." Erik shrugged, then hoisted himself into the back of the truck with her. She wasn't going to make this easy for him, that much was clear. She regarded him with a look that bordered on hostility, reminding him of Regan and of Lynn's admission of her own past.

The image of Lynn, young and bitter and defiant, slipped easily past the pompous attitude he'd shown her earlier and touched his heart in a very tender spot. There was a story to her past, a reason for the rebellious teenager she had been and the cynical adult she had grown into. He wanted to know that story. He wanted to understand. He wanted her to confide in him, wanted to hold her and soothe her as she told him about her troubled youth. But he was going to have to win the right to do that. He doubted she was even going to let him near enough to apologize right now.

She picked up a brown carton labeled LYNN'S OFFICE and thrust it at him. He handed it to one of the volunteers from the Women's Shelter. They worked side by side for an hour without exchanging a word, the chanting of the protestors their only accompaniment. When the back of the truck was empty, Lynn hopped down and started for the cab.

"Is there more stuff at the old house?" Erik asked, falling into step beside her.

"No. This was the last of it. I have to return the truck."

"I'll ride along with you."

Lynn lifted a brow as the Channel 10 news van turned onto the block. "And miss a golden opportunity to tell the public how you've always been deeply concerned about the problems of America's youth?"

Erik bit his lip and pulled the door of the

truck open. "I'll even let you drive," he offered, swallowing the retort that had sprung instantly to his tongue. He deserved the shot, he thought as he cast a slightly longing look at the news van. The politician in him would have liked the publicity, but if he wanted to win Lynn Shaw's respect he would have to forgo the opportunity.

Not waiting for her to agree or disagree, he climbed into the cab and slid across the seat to the passenger side. Lynn got in after him, casting him sideways glances as she started the truck and put it in gear. They rumbled down the tree-lined street, turned the corner, and headed toward Broadway with an ominous grinding of gears.

"It's not that I don't appreciate the help," Lynn said grudgingly, her conscience finally winning out over her stubbornness. "It's the sentiment behind it I'm not so sure about."

"I know."

She shot him a look of annoyance as they pulled up to a stop light and waited. "That's all you have to say — 'I know'?"

Erik's broad shoulders rose and fell. His gaze locked on hers with that magnetic quality that still unnerved her. "Talk hasn't gotten me very far with you," he admitted. "I've decided to let my actions speak for me. I gave a lot of thought to what you said this morning. You were right about some of it. In my own defense, I have to say that I don't usually have the opportunity to get very deeply involved in a cause. There are too many of them and too little time."

"But we're going to be the privileged exception?" Lynn said dryly, turning her attention back to the street as traffic began to move. She gritted her teeth and wrestled the big steering wheel around, the truck lurching and groaning as it heaved around the corner and onto Rochester's main downtown drag.

"I want to prove to you I can care about something besides my own popularity polls," Erik said, raising his voice to be heard above the horrible noises coming from under the moving van's hood.

"You don't have to prove anything to me, Senator." Lynn was careful not to look at him as she spoke, certain he would be wearing that expression of utter sincerity that kept suckering her in. Puppies could have taken lessons from him for heart-melting looks. She glanced out her side window instead, catching a glimpse of the latest fashions in the windows of the elegant Centerplace Galleria building.

"Besides," she said, "isn't that a contradiction? If you care, you care. If you're only doing it to prove something to me, then that negates the rest of it, doesn't it?"

"No. I *want* to care. I want to help you, and by helping you, come to understand the problems your girls are facing. Proving myself to you is a separate issue."

"And unnecessary," Lynn declared. She didn't want him proving himself to her. She didn't want to be the object of a quest.

She hit the blinker and steered the truck onto Seventh Street, bracing herself so hard her fanny came up off the seat. She bit back the groan of effort, but didn't even try to contain her sigh of relief as they completed the turn and she was able to relax again.

"Now I know how truck drivers have room for all those tattoos," she said. "I can feel my biceps growing even now."

"Want me to drive?" Erik queried.

"No."

He chuckled to himself and shook his head. "I didn't think so. You have to do everything the hard way, don't you? No delegating, no passing the buck, no shortcuts."

"I don't like being indebted to people, that's all."

"Afraid of how they'll want to collect?"

Too many debts incurred, she thought, an old hollow ache throbbing anew in her chest. Debts she couldn't ever hope to pay off for sins she wished she hadn't committed. The weight of her past pressed down on her, feeling somehow heavier than usual, the regret that accompanied it more bittersweet. She didn't allow herself to wonder why.

She stomped on the clutch, wrestled the gearshift into position with much protest from the truck, and hauled the wheel hard right, turning into the parking lot of the rental place. The truck bucked up over the lip of the driveway, slamming Erik into the passenger door and window with a thud, and jolted and rattled its way across the gravel lot. Lynn stood on the brakes and the truck rolled on like a horse with a bit between its teeth, finally coming to a grudging halt behind the rental office where all its *compadres* were parked.

Lynn turned off the ignition and fell back against the seat, winded and drained from the physical effort of driving and from the emotional tension of having Erik so near and knowing she couldn't allow him any nearer. She stared out the windshield, pensively watching the clouds of dust they'd kicked up floating away toward John Marshall High School.

Erik watched her as he sat absently rubbing the side of his head where he'd connected with the window. She seemed a million miles away, the weariness in her eyes old and sad. Almost certainly she had somehow fallen back into the past. Erik wanted to reach out to her and pull her back to the present and into his arms. But when he reached for her, she flung open the truck's door and shied away, sliding down out of the cab.

Sighing heavily, he climbed out of the truck and caught up with her beside a formation of small orange rental trailers. They were still behind the green cinderblock office building, well back from the street. This part of town was an unattractive combination of industrial and retail developments put up in the sixties with little consideration for taste. The area around them was fenced in by chain link, with weeds sprouting everywhere there wasn't gravel or a pothole. The afternoon had remained as gray as the morning. The wind had kicked up a bit, hinting at a chance for rain later. It tossed Lynn's long black hair behind her like ribbons and molded her lavender T-shirt to her small, round breasts.

This was hardly the time or the place, but Erik caught himself just wanting to stare at her, to drink in the sight of her. She might have seen that in his eyes because her brows dropped into a scowl and she tried to step around him. He cut her off, boxing her in between himself and a trailer.

"Everyone gets a second chance but me, is that it?" he said, dropping his hands to the waistband of his jeans.

Her lush, pretty mouth pulled down at the corners and she folded her arms defensively. "I don't know what you mean."

"Maybe I'd stand a better chance if I'd spent time in juvenile hall for stealing cars or if I had a little problem with cocaine. Would that make it all right? Could I maybe get you to go out to dinner with me then?"

Lynn refused to take the bait. She'd counseled herself on the issue of Erik Gunther all night and half the day, turning the questions over and back in her mind, always coming up with the same solution: She couldn't afford to get involved with him.

"I told you, I don't mix business and my personal life," she said, congratulating herself for her cool.

"I think your business *is* your personal life," Erik retorted, his hold on his temper slipping a little.

She lifted her chin, green eyes glittering. "You don't know anything about me, Senator."

"I'm trying to remedy that situation, but you won't let me. You're too busy playing the reverse snob."

Lynn's jaw dropped. "Me? I am —"

"You're looking down that pretty nose at me because I'm a politician, because I come from a normal family and had an uneventful adolescence," Erik charged angrily.

This afternoon wasn't working out at all the way he'd planned. He had thought to woo Lynn slowly and calmly as he proved himself to her, but it was fast becoming evident that where Lynn Shaw was concerned he had little control over her or himself. She provoked him in ways he hadn't even considered before. Now he found a well of righteous indignation boiling up inside him and he couldn't seem to stem the flow, regardless of what prudence dictated.

"I came to help you, dammit," he said. "Maybe my motives were only ninety-nine percent pure, but it's a hell of a lot more help than you're getting from anyone else. And maybe I don't understand everything you or your girls have gone through, but you're not giving me much of a chance to, either."

He was right. Lynn looked up at him, wishing she could deliver a scathing rebuttal, but there wasn't one to give. She wasn't being any fairer to him than he had been in his assessment of Regan that morning. And while two wrongs might have kept her safe, they didn't make a right.

She bit her lip and looked off across the ugly plane of the parking lot, where a Minnesota version of a tumbleweed was skittering along. The sky above the Highway 52 overpass was growing heavier with the promise of rain. The sounds of early-rush-hour traffic hummed in the distance. She felt caught between a rock and a hard place, with a minefield spread out around her for good measure. She needed Erik's help, but she didn't need a heartache. Her sense of justice demanded she give him a chance to learn and to care, while her sense of caution told her to keep her distance.

"Come on, Lynn," he said softly. "Give me a break here, will you? I want to do the right thing."

The gravel crunched beneath his sneakers as he shuffled nearer, closing the distance between them. Lynn felt his approach as clearly as she heard it. Her body had tuned in to his the first time he'd come within two feet of her. Standing there, bracing herself against retreat, she had the odd and terrible feeling that she would be acutely aware of Erik Gunther for the rest of her life. She almost flinched when he lifted a hand and gently brushed her hair back from her cheek.

"Come on, Lynn," he whispered. "Give me a chance."

Despite the heat of the day, Lynn shivered. One look at his face told her he was asking for something more than an opportunity to spar with Elliot Graham on her behalf. But it wasn't his entreaty that frightened her. It was the powerful, painful need inside her to say yes. To let him get that close would be the height of folly — for both of them. But she looked up into those Nordic-blue eyes and wanted . . . wanted so much, so badly. To be free of her past, free to have the kind of future that could include a man like Erik.

*Silly,* the cynic in her sneered, sending her tender heart back into hiding. He wasn't asking for a future, he was asking for a date. He was asking for a chance to prove himself by helping her. She would have to have been a fool to turn that down.

"You want your chance, Senator Gunther?" she said, her eyes sliding away from his to the green cinder-block rental office building. "Fine. You've got it."

This wasn't quite what I had in mind, Erik thought two nights later as he hoisted a drapery rod into place above the living room window. He'd been given his "chance," all right — his chance to do manual labor from sunup to sundown. Lynn had worked him like a horse and watched him like a hawk, gauging his every word and action. She had let him prove himself with a hammer and nails, had used his interaction with the girls as a measure of his character. But, whether by chance or design, he hadn't been given much of an opportunity to woo her.

They hadn't had a moment alone. The days had been filled with work and worry, getting things settled in the house and dealing with the problems being laid on Horizon by Elliot Graham's Citizens for Family Neighborhoods. By the end of each day Lynn had looked so exhausted, Erik hadn't had the heart to pursue her. His libido had taken a backseat to the need to simply comfort and hold her, but he hadn't had the chance to do that either. It was getting damned frustrating.

He shot a look at her over his shoulder. "How's this?"

Lynn stood back rubbing her chin, her expression grave as she considered the question of the drapery rod. She looked fresh and pretty in an apricot tank top and a filmy summer skirt that blossomed with blue and peach flowers. A wide leather belt accented her small waist and a pair of fine gold necklaces drew his gaze to the delicate hollow of her throat. This was the first time he'd seen her in something other than jeans and a T-shirt. The effect was wreaking havoc on his hormones.

"A little higher on the left," she pronounced at last, shouting to be heard above the rock music blasting out of the boom box on the coffee table. Erik inched the rod up. She narrowed her eyes in scrutiny. Lillian was called into consultation. Tracy and Michelle joined the audience.

"I like it there."

"I think it was better before."

"I think the senator has a cute butt."

Michelle and Tracy fell into giggles at Tracy's proclamation. Erik felt his cheeks heat, but he wiggled his backside at them, drawing another round of giggles. What he hadn't had to endure in the last two days during the course of toting, hammering, reaching, and lifting. The girls had lost whatever initial shyness they'd had and had progressed to teasing him the way they would have a big brother. His embarrassment threshold had been sorely trod upon, his male ego poked and prodded relentlessly.

His initial reaction had been an inclination to sternness, a desire to reprimand, but he'd held himself in check. This was Lynn's territory, and she had raked him up one side and down the other the one time he had dared challenge her authority. Instead of asserting himself, he had decided to look at this as a test of his tolerance and an opportunity to gain insight into on-the-job sexual harassment.

He gritted his teeth as the muscles in his shoulders began to cramp, and he shot another look at Lynn. "Will this decision be made anytime in the next millennium? I'm hungry."

"You're always hungry," Lynn countered, a wry smile curling one corner of her mouth. "It's a good thing Horizon isn't a home for boys. We'd go broke buying groceries."

"Just for that, I'm ordering double dessert."

"I have no objections, since you're

picking up the tab."

Lynn turned toward her residents. Erik had done plenty of observing in the past two days, and one thing he'd noticed right away was that Lynn almost always tried to include the girls in the decision-making. He had questioned the practice at first, but he'd quickly seen the wisdom of it. Giving the girls a voice in where the furniture went made them feel more a part of the home than just inmates in it, and debates over various issues taught them valuable communications and thinking skills. And it was done so skillfully, so matter-of-factly, Erik doubted the girls realized what was happening. His admiration for Lynn was growing even more quickly than his desire. That surprised him a little, humbled him a lot.

Lynn turned toward the sofa, where Regan was sprawled in insolent repose, her arms crossed tightly over her chest and her combat boots on the table. "Regan?"

The girl's expression was the consummate look of teenage boredom. "Who gives a rip?"

Lynn made no comment, but bent over and turned down the radio as Regan pushed herself to her feet and began roaming restlessly around the room. Lynn turned next to Christine Rickman, the painfully shy, very pregnant fifteen-year-old with honey-blond hair and big brown eyes. "Christine?"

The girl blushed a bit, a tiny smile curving her mouth. She glanced up at Erik but her eyes darted quickly back down and her blush deepened. "I don't know."

Tracy elbowed Michelle and said, "I think the senator should put his rod wherever he wants."

Lynn arched a brow in silent reproach.

The doorbell rang and Erik groaned as Lillian went to answer it. "I don't think this vote needs a quorum. *Somebody* make a decision!"

"Nail it to the wall, Erik," Martha called from where she knelt on the floor with Barbara, sorting through stacks of books.

Barbara groaned. Tracy and Michelle burst into another round of giggles.

"Oh, my, it's so good to hear laughter after the day I've had, I can tell you," Father Bartholomew said. He followed Lillian into the room, wringing his hands and looking his usual disheveled self. A spike of brown hair stuck straight out from the left side of his head. Behind his crooked glasses, his eyes were bright with worry, and there was a telltale flush of color on his cheekbones. "I spent most of the day in Winona, with Bishop Lawrence bending my ear but good."

Lynn's heart gave a lurch as she turned toward the priest. "What did he have to say?"

"Plenty. God love him, he's a wonderful man, but he can get on such a tear. Oh, my, you just don't know." Hands folded against his belly, he rolled his eyes heavenward and offered up a few muttered words in Latin.

"He's seen Graham's petitions?" Lynn asked.

"Yes, and the news on television and in the papers." He flashed Lynn a look of apology. "And I'm afraid I had to tell him about the refrigerator."

"Of course."

"Though I assured him it was not your fault at all, Lynn, dear. He wasn't a happy man, but I managed to work the news in nicely with the biblical story of casting the first stone. He thought it would make an excellent homily." His face lit briefly with a glow of pride.

"What did he have to say about Horizon House?" Erik asked. He lowered the drapery rod and left it balancing on the step stool as he gave his full attention to the priest.

Father Bartholomew gave a dramatic little sigh. His brows pulled together above his nose in a worried peak. He shoved his glasses into place and tried in vain to straighten them. "Well, he's none too pleased with me about letting the house out without the permission of the parish council, but he's backing me up for the moment."

"Thank God," Lillian intoned, one hand worrying the pearls at the collar of her crisp summer-print dress.

"Indeed we should," Father Bartholomew said, nodding enthusiastically. His forehead crinkled and he sucked in a little gasp of air as he shuddered at the memory of the afternoon he'd just spent cloistered with the bishop. "Oh, my, we went around and around about it. I feel like I've been wrestling a bear. He agrees with me that as Christians we are obliged to offer help and refuge, but he's not too crazy about the bad publicity. Pardon me, Senator, but he really doesn't want the diocese to get embroiled in anything political just now."

"But he's letting us stay," Lynn said, sounding more positive than she felt.

Father Bartholomew bobbed his head. "For the time being. We should all pray for the commotion to die down quickly. I don't like to think what he'd do if there got to be too much trouble going on in the neighborhood."

Lynn looked out the curtainless front window at the protestors parading up and down the sidewalk, led by none other than Elliot Graham himself, looking proper and upstanding in his shirt and tie. Her stomach slid a little. If Graham had his way, the commotion would not die down. And if the bishop threw them out of this house, it might well mean the end of Horizon. The only other building they'd been able to find was an empty county services office building located in the floodplain along the Zumbro River. Access to it had been denied "for safety reasons," they'd been informed that very afternoon when she and Lillian had gone downtown to the courthouse to check on it.

Erik put a hand on Lynn's shoulder and gave a little squeeze of reassurance. It was far less than he wanted to do, but he didn't think taking her in his arms and kissing her in front of Father Bartholomew, the girls, and Elliot Graham's band would be advisable or appreciated.

"I've made a few phone calls," he said. "I haven't gotten a lot of feedback yet, but

I hope to hear something in a day or two that could be of help. In the meantime, I'm offering dinner. How about it, Father? All the pizza you can eat and antacid floats for dessert."

The priest perked up at the sound of that, but his expression quickly slid into hesitancy. "Oh, my, well, that sounds like fun, but I don't know if I should —"

"Aw, come on," Erik prodded, his heart going out to the priest. Father Bartholomew was like a mouse taking on a lion. Erik admired the man for finding the courage to stand up for his beliefs. There weren't many people willing to do that these days. "In for a penny, in for a pound, as they say. Besides," he joked, flashing the priest a sheepish grin, "I need another man around. All these females intimidate me."

Father Bartholomew wrung his hands, visibly screwing up his determination. "Well . . . all right," he said with a nod and a gleam of adventure in his eyes.

"Let's go, gang," Erik announced. "My rod can wait," he said, straight-faced, looking straight at Tracy and Michelle. "My stomach can't."

The girls choked on their giggles. Lynn chuckled and shook her head as she let Erik usher her toward the door with a hand at the small of her back. Lillian helped Christine up from her chair, Martha struggled to her feet and lumbered after them, scooping her purse from the coffee table and turning off the boom box.

At the front door, Lynn jerked herself to a halt and looked sharply around, brows drawing together. "Where's Regan?"

"I don't know."

"She was here a minute ago."

Their departure was delayed as Lynn and Lillian made a quick search of the house. Regan was nowhere to be found.

"She must have slipped out through the back while we were talking," Erik said, biting his tongue on any further comment. While the other girls at Horizon had managed to melt his reserve toward them, Regan had made no effort. In fact, she seemed bent on antagonizing him. He couldn't seem to stop himself from thinking the girl was a brat deluxe who needed a good spanking more than anything else. But he kept that opinion to himself.

"Well," Lynn said with a shrug, "she loses out on the fun."

She didn't like the idea of letting Regan go off on her own, but she liked the idea of tracking her down and dragging her back

141

home even less. Force wasn't the key to knocking down Regan's defenses. She only hoped the girl came around emotionally before she got herself into more trouble.

"I'm glad we decided to walk," Lynn said, stuffing her hands into the deep pockets of her skirt. The entourage had jockeyed around until she had gotten shuffled to the back of the pack — with Erik. The girls had decided Erik was cool, and they were being none too subtle in their efforts to pair their counselor off with him. Lynn caught the furtive, bright-eyed looks being snuck back over shoulders at her, and a smile pulled at her lips.

"Me too," Erik said on a long sigh. He patted his stomach. "I need to walk off those last ten slices of pizza."

Evening was sliding into night. The sun was sinking beyond the trees to the west, spilling its last few drops of warm orange light across the placid surface of Silver Lake. The park on the small lake's banks was dotted with people out for evening strolls with their dogs, feeding cracked corn to the hundreds of big Canada geese who made the lake their year-round home.

The crowd was thinning as darkness descended. Soon the lake would be moonlit and the park benches would be empty, inviting lovers to sit and gaze up at the stars. The romantic thought slipped through Lynn's wall of hard practicality before she had a chance to squelch it, making her even more acutely aware of the man beside her.

His stride was slow and relaxed, as if he didn't care if it took until midnight to get back. He had his hands stuffed in the pockets of his jeans, snugging the fabric against his maleness. Lynn felt her cheeks heat as her gaze caught ever so briefly on that masculine bulge. She cleared her throat and tried to quicken her pace, but Erik lagged back and the girls rushed on ahead, herding Martha and Lillian and Father Bartholomew with them. She was left with the choice of running to catch up with them, or behaving like a calm, rational adult and staying in step with the senator.

Feeling neither calm nor rational, she deliberately slowed her pace. They were on a public thoroughfare. What could possibly happen?

*I could fall for him.*

The answer came without a second's hesitation, sending goose bumps chasing over her skin despite the warm summer evening. She had spent the last two days testing him, cynically certain he would fail.

But he hadn't. Erik had passed her tests with flying colors. He had worked without complaint, suffered the teasing of her girls, given unselfishly of his time and his talents. He'd spent tireless hours on the phone trying to drum up support for Horizon House. Not once had he tried to capitalize publicly on his efforts. His name was displayed prominently in the articles and reports about Horizon's situation, but he wasn't actively seeking out reporters or calling news conferences as she had expected him to do.

He had offered her his aid, his encouragement, his strength. Lynn had told herself she would be a fool to turn him down. She had told herself she would be able to take what he was willing to give coolly and cynically, without her heart becoming involved at all. But as she'd watched his stiffness with the girls melt away into genuine caring, she'd felt her cynicism about Erik Gunther melt too. The one buffer that had kept her safe from falling into something foolish was crumbling around her like a stale cookie.

A burst of laughter floated back from the group ahead of them and penetrated Lynn's trance. Tracy and Barbara broke into song, then giggles.

"They're really pretty good kids, aren't they?" Erik said, not quite able to keep all the astonishment out of his voice.

Lynn smiled gently as he ducked his head and flashed her a sheepish look. "They have problems. They've made mistakes. But they're good kids. They're trying hard to get their lives back on track."

"Except Regan."

"She'll come around."

"Do they all?"

No, Lynn thought. She'd lost the battle more than once. Each time it happened it broke her heart, but sometimes it was an inevitability. She couldn't reach every girl, no matter how badly she wanted to, no matter how hard she tried. But she wouldn't lose Regan, she vowed. She couldn't lose Regan. Regan was like looking into a mirror and seeing herself fifteen years ago, hurting, bitter, afraid, wanting people to care but batting their hand away every time they reached out to help.

"I don't like this disappearing act of hers, Lynn," Erik said. "If she gets into trouble it's going to come down on Horizon like a ton of bricks. Right now public support outside the neighborhood is running slightly in your favor, but that pendulum can swing overnight."

"I know," Lynn admitted glumly. "I'm going to have a talk with her tomorrow."

"Yeah, if she's around," he muttered sarcastically. "Maybe she'll even listen."

Lynn bristled instantly, stopping in her tracks and glaring at him. "If you don't like the way I'm doing my job —"

"Whoa!" Erik held up a hand to cut her off. "I never said —"

"You implied —"

"I did not." He reined back what seemed to be a natural urge to spar with her and took a deep breath to calm himself.

It was amazing. He had never been the argumentative sort with his dates. With Lynn he actually enjoyed debating whatever issue was at hand, whether it was politics or pizza — not in an angry way, just debating. He liked seeing that green fire in her eyes, enjoyed her sharp wit, cared about what she had to say. Caring. That was the key, he realized with a jolt. What he felt for Lynn Shaw went beyond what he'd ever felt for any other woman. He'd known that from the first night, but it still startled him every time it hit him anew.

"Look," he said, settling his hands on her rigid shoulders. "Let's not fight. Let's not talk business. It's time to turn our attention to more enjoyable things."

Lynn looked up at him warily, taking in the soft light in his eyes, the secretive smile canting his mouth. His fingers moved gently on the bare skin of her shoulders, igniting fires deep inside. When he looked at her that way she got the feeling he knew everything good about the world, that he could shelter her from the bad, lift her up to a plane where only the two of them existed and no one could ever touch them or hurt them. She wanted to be mesmerized, wanted to be drawn in, wanted to let Sir Erik the Good sweep her away into the sunset. And that scared the hell out of her.

She cast a nervous glance at the rest of their group, now a distant moving knot of color.

"Let them go," Erik said softly. "I want some time alone with you."

"And do you always get what you want, Senator?"

He grinned. "If I work hard and live right."

Lynn gave a little sniff of derision, but she let him take her hand and lead her off the sidewalk and down the slope to a park bench. The bench was tucked between the bank of the lake and a bower of pine trees and lilac bushes, isolated from the main park area and partially secluded. What few people remained in the park were oblivious to them, giving Lynn the fanciful feeling that this was an enchanted spot reserved for white knights. She chided herself for being foolish as she sat down and arranged her skirt around her. It had been a very long time since she'd believed in enchantment; she wasn't about to trust in it.

Erik settled in beside her, stretching his arms along the back of the bench so she either had to touch him or perch herself on the edge of the seat like a skittish virgin. Her heart boomed in her chest like thunder as she eased herself back and allowed him to curl his fingers around her shoulder.

"Relax," he whispered, shifting his position deftly so that Lynn found herself suddenly snuggled against his side.

She looked up at him with wry amusement. "That was slick. I'll bet you caught a lot of cheerleaders unawares with that move back in high school."

"Naw." He looked across the lake, the expression in his eyes a little wistful. "I didn't have a lot of time for dating back then. I worked nights and weekends. It was either that or miss out on college. I was counting on a scholarship or two, but that doesn't pay for everything. . . ." His voice trailed away, as if the memory of those times cost him too much. After a moment of silence, he flashed her an endearing little smile and said, "Besides, I was kind of shy around girls."

"You? Shy?" Lynn laughed her disbelief. She'd never known anyone as solidly self-assured as Erik. The image of him as a big coltish teenager baffled by his appeal to girls tugged at her heart. He must have been too cute for words. And his shyness would only have made matters worse for him, drawing girls like a magnet, the poor kid.

"What about you?" he asked, turning the tables on her. "What were you like at seventeen?"

"Me?" It was Lynn's turn to stare off across the darkening lake. "Every man with a daughter has nightmares about girls like I was."

She stopped herself from saying more. The memories were there as always, but beneath the surface, dark and unhappy, and a part of her wanted to let them out. She had kept her past bottled inside her for so long. It was a constant pressure in her chest, waiting to be released, but always she held it back, clinging to it, hiding it. A part of her wanted to confide in Erik, to lean on him, to unburden herself. He was so big and so solid and so strong. But he was also good and pure and she could easily see the disillusionment and disappointment that would come into his eyes. He had softened his attitude toward her girls, but that new understanding was a fragile coating over old judgmental attitudes. They would have only the summer together as it was, then Erik would be back in St. Paul, on to other issues and other causes and the business of running the state. What was the point in spoiling the time they had?

"It's a long, sad story," she whispered, wrapping her arms around herself to ward off a shiver. "You don't want to hear it."

"I do." He bent his head and brushed his lips against her temple. "I want to know everything about you."

Lynn shook her head, her gaze still focused on the middle distance. The gracefully arched limestone footbridge across the way was holding the last faint glow of dusk. The water below had already gone dark and glassy. The sky to the east was velvet black above the dense forest of Quarry Hills.

"Kiss me," Erik ordered, his voice so soft Lynn thought for a moment she'd imagined it.

Pulling away from her past, she looked up at him and managed a little laugh. "I thought you were shy."

Erik slid his hand up to the back of her neck and lowered his mouth toward hers. "I got over it."

Lynn tilted her face up to receive his kiss, letting her eyes flutter closed, letting her past drift away. She didn't want the burden of it any longer. She wanted this — the feel of Erik's arms sliding around her, the taste of him invading her mouth, the sensation of being overwhelmed by the power of his magnetism and sexuality. She wanted this to be her world for just a moment or two. She wanted to think of nothing else, not the girls or the house or anything beyond the two of them sitting here beside the lake sharing a kiss.

She gave herself over to him. Her tongue arched gently against his as she allowed him access to the warm sweetness of her mouth. A delicate shiver trickled down her spine from where his fingers kneaded the nape of her neck and settled at the base in a feathery sensation that made her shiver all over again. The delicious heat of desire flowed through her like sun-warmed honey, swirling in her breasts, pooling in the aching emptiness of her femininity. It had been forever since she'd let a man touch her this way, so long that he seemed like the first. Every sensation seemed new and intense, crackling along her nerves like electricity.

His right hand slid up from the curve of her waist to cradle a breast, squeezing gently in a rhythm that echoed the thrust of his tongue. Lynn whimpered and arched into his touch, losing her breath as his thumb flicked slowly back and forth across her nipple, bringing the sensitive nub to aching attention. She tried to press herself closer to him and Erik took advantage, trailing kisses down the exposed column of her throat.

The heat of sexual need was burning away every ounce of sense Erik had. He was dimly aware of the fact that they were in a public park, but thoughts of being discovered were being shoved to the back of his mind by the all-consuming desire to make love to Lynn. He wanted to lay her down in the grass and kiss and caress every inch of her. He wanted to see her breasts by moonlight and suckle them until she begged him for release. He wanted to gather her beneath him and ease himself into the tight warmth of her woman's sheath, claiming her in a mating ritual as old as time.

Primitive. That was the base of what he was feeling. The primitive male urge to bond with a female, body and soul. And overlaying those basic instincts was the need to comfort, to ease the pain he'd seen in her eyes when she'd been lost in thoughts of the past.

He whispered her name and stroked a hand over her hair, framed her face with his hands and pressed kisses to her eyelids and cheeks, trailed one hand down her throat and lingered at the fragile hollow where her pulse fluttered like a bird's wing.

"So sweet," he whispered, each word a kiss. "So sweet."

Lynn tipped her chin up, seeking his mouth again, craving the taste of him. She pressed a hand against his chest, glorying in the feel of solid muscle and the hard steady pounding of his heart. Then Erik's fingers closed around her wrist and guided her down over the taut plane of his belly to where his erection strained against the front of his jeans. She groaned as he molded her fingers around his shaft, letting her feel the size and shape of him, the strength of his desire for her. His tongue began a slow, suggestive thrust against hers once again and Lynn's temperature soared.

She was burning up wanting him. The sexuality she had suppressed for so long was unfurling inside her, coming to life like a desert flower that had lain dormant waiting for rain. The feelings were over-whelming, wild, whirling through her like a strong, hot wind. She pulled her mouth from his and gasped for air as his hand found its way under her skirt and swept up her thigh to the warm, damp juncture of her legs. Her strongest desire was to open up to him. She wanted the feel of his fin-gers slipping inside her panties to stroke her silken heat, to caress the aching petals of her femininity, to probe and touch the core of her desire. But some small grain of sanity remained beneath the haze of pas-sion, irritating her, prodding her to come to her senses.

"No," she whispered breathlessly, her hand sliding from the front of his jeans to stop his progress. Her fingers curled around his wrist and it was all she could do to keep from guiding him to her instead of away. "No," she repeated, as much to con-vince herself as him.

Need burned like a blue flame in Erik's

eyes as he looked down at her. Night had fallen around them, casting their private alcove in shadows silvered by the light of a streetlamp standing somewhere behind them. In the stark mix of light and dark he looked strikingly male, his nostrils flaring slightly with each heavy breath, the muscles in his wide, square jaw flexing as he stared down at her.

"Let me take you home tonight, Lynn," he said, his voice a deep, husky rasp.

Lynn met his gaze. She was trembling, she realized dimly. Trembling with need, trembling with fear. Oh, God, she wanted to say yes. She wanted to take him to her bed and let him finish what they'd started here. But if she said yes then they would be taking this relationship to a new level where the stakes were high and the odds were against her. She had told herself a hundred times she couldn't have a relationship with Erik Gunther, but in that moment she couldn't think of many things she'd ever wanted more.

He lifted his hand to her face and brushed his thumb gently against her cheek. The action was infinitely tender, a poignant counterpoint to the raw desire in his expression. Lynn drew in a shallow, shuddering breath.

"Erik, I —"

"Lynn! Lynn!"

Lynn's head snapped around at the strident call. It was an alarm. Dread slammed into her with terrible force, jolting her heart up against her breastbone. She was off the bench in an instant, running toward the sound of Tracy's voice.

"Tracy!"

The girl came running, breathless and wide-eyed, looking as if she'd been chased the whole way by some nightmarish beast. She pulled up just short of Lynn, holding her side and gasping for breath.

Lynn clutched at the girl's shoulders. "Honey, what's wrong? What's happened? Is it Christine? Is the baby coming?"

Tracy shook her head, ponytail swinging. "No. It's not Christine. It's the cops."

# — 7 —

A small crowd stood in Cyrus Johansen's side lawn staring at the four-letter word sprayed in black paint across the wall of the garage. The wall was illuminated by a dozen flashlights, two of them held by Officers Reuter and Briggs.

Elliot Graham stood beside Lynn at the front of the crowd, in his shirt and tie, his fanatic's eyes burning bright with righteousness in the flickering glow of the flashlights. His son hovered behind him, looking sullen, hands stuffed deep into the pockets of a pair of baggy black shorts.

"This is exactly the kind of thing I've been waiting for," the senior Graham said loudly and bitterly.

"Then you're not disappointed, are you?" Lynn muttered half under her breath.

He gave her a sharp look. "What was that, Miss Shaw?"

Erik wedged his way in between them before she could answer. Lynn stepped back reluctantly, resentfully, wanting to take a shot at Graham's pomposity and knowing that Erik was trying to save her from making matters worse. She was upset because of the vandalism, because of Graham, because of the emotional tug-of-war she was waging with herself over Erik. The stage was set for her to react with her feelings instead of her brain, and Erik had sensed that. Or maybe he simply thought no one could handle the situation as well as he could. Either way, it struck Lynn on a pair of raw nerves.

"Before you make an outright accusation, Mr. Graham," Erik said smoothly, "I would point out that there's no signature on that wall."

"It's hardly necessary," Graham snapped. "We've never had this kind of trouble in the neighborhood before."

"The fact remains, you don't have any proof that this was done by one of the Horizon residents."

"How much proof do you need?" Graham's son sneered sarcastically.

Erik pierced the boy with a stern, cold look that would have made a Minnesota winter seem balmy by comparison. "More than your personal prejudices, young man."

The boy scowled and scuttled back farther behind his father.

To Lynn's right, Cyrus and Edna Johansen were standing with Reuter and Briggs, giving their statement. "Edna and me had just set down to watch the news when we heard this commotion. . . ."

"Oh, my," Father Bartholomew groaned, wringing his hands. His worried gaze darted from the Johansens to Lynn, then to Graham and back to Lynn again. "I don't want to think what the bishop is going to have to say about this," he mumbled for her ears only.

Lynn wanted to point out that anyone might have done the deed. Rochester certainly had more problem youths than just those living at Horizon. Vandalism was not an uncommon problem. But she said nothing. The fact was, it wasn't going to matter to Bishop Lawrence who had done the deed. What would matter to him would be the negative light cast on St. Stephen's. Speculation that one of the Horizon girls had done this would be enough to make him unhappy.

"This is exactly the kind of thing that happens when you welcome delinquents into a neighborhood," Graham droned on.

"We were hardly welcomed," Lynn snapped, turning on her adversary, her temper fraying down to the nub. She leaned around Erik to glare at the man.

"Nor should you have been," Graham said, lifting his nose to a superior angle. "The families living here don't want to be subjected to this kind of upheaval," he said. Then, gesturing dramatically toward the wall, he added, "Or this kind of language."

"Oh, give me a break —"

"Lynn." Erik turned toward her with a pained smile and took her by the shoulders, steering her back away from Graham. He looked down at her, a plea for common sense plain in his eyes. "Why don't you take everyone to the house and wait? Turning this into a brawl isn't going to help the cause," he said in an anxious whisper.

Lynn frowned at him. It galled her, but she knew he was right. The less hoopla, the better for them. With a few brief words to Lillian and Martha, she turned and led them down the street toward the house, where the girls waited anxiously on the porch steps for some word. Everyone was ushered in. Martha went to the kitchen to brew a pot of tea. Lillian paced the living room, worrying at her pearls. Father Bartholomew sank into an armchair, looking like a reluctant martyr. The girls hovered in a knot in the doorway, their eyes on Lynn as she stood at the front window looking out.

"They're going to get rid of us, aren't they?" Barbara said.

Tracy's eyes narrowed angrily. "We didn't do anything. They're nothing but a bunch of jerks."

Lynn sighed and walked across the room to the girls, reaching up wearily to tuck a loose strand of hair behind her ear as she went. "Don't lump them all into that category, honey," she said wearily. "They're not all bad. No more than all kids with problems are bad."

Tracy's mouth fell into a pout and she glanced away. Lynn's gaze moved over the quartet, settling on Christine. The girl held one hand pressed to her rounded belly. Her dark eyes were enormous and shining with worry as she turned toward Lynn.

"I'm scared," she whispered in a tiny voice.

Lynn slid an arm around her and squeezed her shoulders. "Don't worry, sweetie. We'll pull through this." She flashed them all a grin she didn't feel. "We've got Senator Hunk on our side."

"Yeah. All they have is Elliot Graham,"

Michelle said, grinding out his name as if it left a bad taste in her mouth.

"And that weird geek kid of his," Tracy added. "Have you seen that guy?" She gave a shudder of disgust. "He gives me the creeps."

As Lynn ushered the girls upstairs to their rooms, the conversation gravitated from geeks to hunks to Erik. She found herself blushing a little as they probed for details of the time she'd spent alone with him at the lake.

"We sat and talked," she hedged, dodging Michelle's inquisitive gaze as she turned down the covers on a bed.

"Yeah, right," Tracy said, chuckling wickedly as she dragged a brush through her mop of burnished brown curls.

"He's *sooo* cute," Barbara groaned, leaning against the doorjamb in her night-gown as if the mere thought of him sapped the strength from her knees.

Lynn plumped one last pillow, then stood back with her hands on her hips, regarding the girls with a serious expression. "Look, I know you guys think Senator Gunther is choice, but don't look for too much to come out of this. Erik is a busy man, and I don't have time for a relation-ship either. We're enjoying each other's company for a while, but that's all."

Tracy slanted her a look as she settled on the bed and crossed her legs yoga fashion. "Really, Lynn, you ought to have more to your life than just us."

That sage comment hit Lynn like a brick and rocked her back on her feet a bit. *Out of the mouths of babes . . .* She recovered with an effort. "Maybe when we're out of danger of being thrown into the street," she said dryly.

She bid the girls good night and trudged slowly back down the stairs, not eager to deal with the police — or Erik, for that matter. Tracy's words echoed in her head and she seized on them, diverting herself from one problem with another.

She *didn't* have a life outside Horizon. Even though she didn't live here, this was her home and these people were her family. Martha and Lillian were her friends, but they were also surrogate mothers. The girls were residents, here for her to help through counseling, but they were also her foster daughters, the children she didn't have. They afforded her the chance to be a mother without running the risk of a romantic involvement.

For a long time she had been perfectly content with those roles and the feelings

163

that accompanied them. She had broken her relationship with her own family beyond repair. She had taken her shot at romance long ago and had been betrayed utterly. Her second chance at family life had been delivered to her in the form of Horizon House, and she had accepted it gratefully as more than she deserved. But suddenly she caught herself wanting something else. . . .

"They've promised not to use thumbscrews. You don't have to look quite so doomed."

Erik's voice jolted Lynn from her thoughts. He took her by the hand as she moved away from the stairs, then led her slowly toward the living room, where the two police officers were sitting on the sofa sipping Martha's tea and eating Fig Newtons. Lynn did her best to ignore the tingles racing up her arm, did her best not to think about how warm and strong his hand was around hers.

"Did you get yourself on the news, Senator?" she asked, sending him a wry smile.

Erik shook his head. "There isn't a crew to be had at that station this time of night," he muttered, his mouth drawn into a grim line and a little crease of concern digging in between his eyebrows. "But Graham will have them out here first thing in the morning. You can bet on that."

They took their places on chairs that had been dragged in from the dining room. Lillian refused to sit, her nervous energy propelling her around the room like a butterfly flitting from perch to perch. Martha and Father Bartholomew occupied the two overstuffed chairs, looking like a pair of giant gloom-and-doom bookends.

Lynn regarded the officers carefully. They would side with Graham. Police had a natural suspicion of teenagers, especially those who had track records of trouble. It would also make their job much easier if they could simply pin this on one of her girls and close the case. The idea brought her protective instincts rushing to the fore, and she took the offensive without a second's hesitation.

"Our girls didn't do this."

"You can account for them at the time of the incident?" Officer Briggs asked. He tried to discreetly dust cookie crumbs from his mustache, then took up his notepad and pencil.

"We had just returned from dinner out," Lillian said, hovering momentarily behind Lynn.

"You were all out together?"

Erik turned to Lynn, bracing himself for her reaction. "Everyone except Regan," he said hesitantly.

Lynn couldn't have looked more hurt if he'd slapped her. She stared at him, feelings of betrayal written plainly across her delicate features. Erik cursed himself for being too honest, and he cursed Regan for being such a source of contention between Lynn and himself. The girl was trouble, no two ways about it, but Lynn had a blind spot where Regan was concerned, seeing too much of herself in the girl.

"Regan didn't do it," Lynn stated baldly, her attention solely on Erik.

"Where is this Regan now?" Reuter asked.

"She went out on her own earlier," Martha said. "She likes to hang out at Peace Plaza."

"So she could have done it," Briggs said.

Lynn went on glaring at Erik. "But she didn't."

"Pardon me, Miss Shaw, but you have no way of knowing that. We'll want to talk to her tomorrow."

After a few more questions and another cookie each, the officers took their leave, assuring Lynn they would be back in the morning to talk to Regan. Father

Bartholomew followed them out the front door, saying the rosary under his breath as he went.

The house fell as quiet as a tomb as the others turned away from the door and set about the business of getting the living room back in order. Tension and dread hung in the air, amplifying sounds like the rattle of china, the scrape of a chair.

"See anything promising in those tea-cups, Martha?" Erik asked, needing to break the silence.

"I'm afraid to look," she answered glumly, and followed Lillian out to the kitchen.

Left alone with Lynn, Erik leaned against the doorway and watched her carefully as she plumped the couch pillows and brushed crumbs from the cushions. Her lush mouth was set in a fierce line. Hostility rolled off her in waves. He closed his eyes for a second and thought about how good she'd felt in his arms as they'd sat beside Silver Lake. And he wondered how long it would be before he had her in his arms again. When hell froze over, by the look of things.

"We don't know that she didn't do it," he said, wanting to get this fight over with as soon as possible.

Lynn straightened away from the couch, shoulders squared, jaw set, emerald eyes glittering. "We don't know that she did."

"It was certainly a word from her vocabulary," Erik said, pushing himself away from the doorjamb. He pulled his hands from his pockets and propped them on his hips as he took a step toward Lynn.

She advanced a step as well. "It's a word from my vocabulary, too, Senator," she said sarcastically. "And I believe I heard you use it the other day when you hit your thumb with a hammer. Does that mean we should be searching your things for a can of spray paint?"

Erik sighed. He really didn't feel like butting heads. He only wanted her to see reason for once where Regan Mitchell was concerned. "Lynn, I'm not accusing her. I just think you should face the possibility that she might have done it. She hasn't exactly been shy about her feelings. She hates it here. She said she didn't care what happened to Horizon. She could see getting you closed down as a way out."

"You don't understand," Lynn said, calling on the phrase that was the anthem of teenage girls everywhere. But she *did* understand, and she wanted Erik to understand as well. She looked up at him, her

168

expression begging eloquently for her cause. "That's a challenge. Regan wants us to care about her, *really* care, but she's going to make it as tough as possible so she can be sure that it's the real thing."

"Well, she does a bang-up job of that."

"Yeah." Her shoulders sagged under the weight of it all. She wandered past Erik and into the hall, where she leaned against the stair railing and stared up into the darkness of the second floor. "Well," she said wearily, not even sure if he could hear her, "it's a lot easier to be an expert at doing it than an expert at dealing with it."

Erik slid his arms around her waist and hugged her, dropping his head down to press a soft kiss against her temple. "I'll leave that to you. You're damn good at what you do, honey. I just don't want to see you pin your hopes on this kid and have her let you down."

"I don't want that either," she murmured, wishing with all her heart that so much wasn't resting on Regan, because, despite her need to defend the girl, in her heart of hearts she knew there was a chance Erik was right. She turned in his arms and looked up at him, dismissing the subject for the moment. "I suppose you feel compelled to spend the night again, Sir Galahad?"

He nodded gravely.

Lynn made a face. "We've really dragged you into something here, haven't we? I'm sure you'd rather be spending your nights somewhere other than our lumpy couch."

His eyes warmed to a deep, vibrant shade of sapphire. There was no mistaking what he was thinking about as his gaze held hers and a slow smile turned up the corners of his mouth. "Yeah. In fact, I was kind of counting on it tonight."

"I don't know if *you* should pin your hopes on *me,* Senator," she said, regret striking a poignant chord inside her. "I might have to let you down."

"Why?" Erik demanded. His expression changed in the blink of an eye. Suddenly he had the look of a man used to getting answers, a man who didn't settle for anything less than what he was after. "And don't give me that conflict-of-interest crap. We could have something really special, Lynn. We both know it. We both feel it. Why won't you let it happen?"

"It won't work out," she said defensively, digging up every trite-but-true answer she could find. "We're busy people. We're dedicated to our careers —"

"I'm dedicated, but I'm not a slave. You shouldn't be either. You deserve to have a life outside of this house."

The look in Lynn's eyes told him she wasn't sure she did deserve it. Erik wondered what might seed that kind of doubt, but he didn't probe for the answer. When she was ready, she would tell him. Instead, he set himself to the task of railroading her. He was, indeed, a man used to getting what he wanted. Lynn wasn't going to be the exception to the rule.

"Friday night," he said firmly. "We're going out on a real date. You and me. No teenagers. No grandmothers. No excuses."

"But — but what about the house?" Lynn stammered. "What if something happens? What if —"

"Lillian and Martha are perfectly capable of handling things for a few hours. They managed to live sixty-some years without you or me to watch out for them."

She scowled at him. "That's just because they didn't know any better," she muttered crossly.

"Come on, counselor," Erik cajoled, eyes twinkling like stars in the dim light of the hall. "A date. Even us white knights deserve a little time off from the cause once in a while."

171

Lynn looked at him sideways, naturally resistant to being bullied. She told herself she would have walked away from him if it weren't for the fact that he had his arms around her . . . and his thighs pressed to hers . . . and that adorable sparkle in his eyes . . .

A date. One date. He wasn't asking for the moon. He wasn't promising it, either. She closed her eyes for a second and thought back to the way she'd felt as he'd held her in the moonlight by the lake. She ached to feel that way again — whether she deserved it or not. They could have their date. They could have their night together. As long as she knew in her heart that a night or two was all they would have.

"All right, Senator," she conceded, giving him a smile that was unintentionally wistful and a little bit sad. "It's a date."

# — 8 —

Friday was a long time coming.

Lynn had her promised talk with Regan and was less than pleased with the results. Regan accused her once again of caring more about Horizon than her. She flatly refused to reveal her whereabouts the night of the vandalism and was openly hostile to Officers Reuter and Briggs. They scowled at her with jaundiced eyes, but as they had no witnesses and could produce no physical evidence linking Regan with the crime, they had to give her the benefit of the doubt. They made it clear, however, that she was their prime suspect and that they would be keeping tabs on her. This news went over like the proverbial lead balloon, sending Regan into a tantrum. The situation was not improved by the announcement from the Horizon staff that Regan's nocturnal forays would stop.

The girl was furious, but Lynn detected a hint of something else in her mood beneath all the bluster. It might have been panic of a sort. She couldn't quite tell, couldn't quite put her finger on it, but she would have bet her last dime that Regan's nighttime activities consisted of something more than sitting around the Peace Plaza fountain harassing passersby.

She fully expected Regan to rebel and try to leave, but no rebellion ever came. After refusing dinner, Regan spent the evening sequestered in her room in utter, absolute silence.

As Erik had predicted, the News 10 crew, as well as a full complement of newspaper people, had arrived in the neighborhood the morning after the garage incident. Elliot Graham stayed home from work for the occasion, mustering his troops behind him as he stood before the camera and made angry declarations against "the terrible tide of violence against decent people."

It was nearly enough to incite Lynn to violence. The man made it sound as if people weren't safe in their beds at night. And the worst part of it was, there seemed to be more and more people siding with him. The day shift of demonstrators on the sidewalk increased by a dozen or more and the phone rang off the hook with calls from angry citizens blaming Horizon House residents for everything from trampling flower beds to perpetuating the national debt.

By the time Friday night rolled around, Lynn was more than ready for a break from it all. As dedicated as she was to Horizon, the constant strain of the last two weeks was beginning to wear on her. The idea of being swept away from it all for a night held so much appeal it almost scared her.

She dressed for the date with too much care. A very bad sign, the cynic in her sneered as she stood before the mirror in her bedroom. She had fussed too much with her hair, arranging her long, silky black tresses with a pair of mother-of-pearl combs and spritzing her bangs into place. She had taken too long applying her makeup with the painstaking care of an artist, playing up her eyes, accenting her cheekbones, painting her lips a warm, delicious pink. The dress she had chosen was a little too nice — emerald-green silk, sleeveless with a full skirt. Gold-rimmed mother-of-pearl buttons marched down the front from throat to hem and a wide woven belt emphasized her narrow waist.

"You look like you're expecting a proposal," she accused.

Her feelings were a complicated tangle of disgust and dread as she turned from the mirror toward the closet in search of an outfit that didn't look so . . . so . . . *hopeful.* She cringed at the word. This was a date, a night out, a meal with a little interaction afterward, that was all. There was nothing to be hopeful about, she told herself as she flung a blue cotton sundress onto the bed and turned back to the closet to dig for her espadrilles.

The doorbell rang when she was up to her elbows in shoes. Cursing under her breath, she stumbled out of the closet and picked her way across the bedroom, tiptoeing over the discarded dresses that littered the floor. She pulled the door shut behind her and took a deep breath, then forced herself to walk calmly across the living room as the bell chimed again.

Erik stood in the hall looking devastatingly handsome and clutching a small nosegay of violets. He wore a crisp blue dress shirt with a trendy tie and neatly pressed, pleated gray trousers. Lynn actually felt his gaze pour down over her, from the top of her head to the tips of her stockinged toes. Goose bumps raced down her arms as a budding warmth opened in the center of her like a new rose.

"You're beautiful," he murmured, that wise, secretive smile crinkling the corners of his eyes.

Lynn's heart did a somersault in her chest. "You're early," she blurted ungraciously.

Erik grinned at the accusation as he stepped into the apartment. "I didn't want to give you a chance to duck out on me."

"Thanks for the vote of confidence," she said dryly, taking the delicate tissue-wrapped flowers from his grasp. She stepped around the service bar into the tiny yellow kitchen and reached up into the cupboard for a vase. "And thanks for the flowers," she added softly, more touched by the gesture than she wanted to be.

"They were growing wild in the woods behind my house," Erik said. He roamed the living room, searching for personal touches, things that might give him more clues to the lady he found himself falling so hard for. There wasn't much. A nubby-weave, oatmeal-colored sofa and chair. A coffee table buried under neatly arranged stacks of file folders. A wall unit crammed with textbooks, a stereo, and three dying plants in ceramic pots. A framed photo on the television showing her with Lillian, Martha, and a crop of Horizon alumni on a camping trip. He touched a finger to the dusty frame, then turned and shot her a grin. "I'm pretty sure I broke the law picking them."

Lynn gasped and pressed a hand to her heart. "Senator, such scandalous behavior! I hope no one saw you."

"Me too. I was out there in my underwear while my pants were in the dryer."

She laughed, and he felt that warm sliding feeling in his belly. God, she was beautiful. The dress made her eyes look even greener than emeralds. It clung in all the right places, enhancing her femininity. Her face lit up with that inner fire that made her so vibrant, so tenacious, and Erik wanted to take her in his arms right there and then. It took an effort to rein in his desire.

"I'm not too worried," he said, his voice a little huskier than usual as his gaze lingered on her breasts. "I live out in Buckthorn. I think maybe a couple of squirrels saw me." He pulled his eyes off her and gestured to the room at large. "So do I get the grand tour?"

"You're looking at it," Lynn said. She shoved a stack of unopened mail aside and set the flowers in the center of the counter. "You can see the whole apartment from where you're standing."

"I can't see the bedroom," he said, his gaze sliding back to her, dark and glowing with insinuation.

Another burst of warmth showered through Lynn. "Trust me, you don't want to. It looks like a bomb went off at Casual Corner."

"I'll close my eyes."

"Then you won't see much."

"I told you before," he said with a devilish smile, "I'm good with my hands."

"Forget it, hotshot," Lynn drawled, grabbing up her keys. "You promised me a night on the town."

"I *coerced* you into a night on the town."

She shot him a scowl. "Split hairs."

They locked the apartment and walked out of the building into the warm summer night, angling across the parking lot toward Erik's Thunderbird.

"I need to stop by the house for two seconds before we go," Lynn said as she settled into the car's plush seat and Erik slid behind the wheel. He gave her a look of strained patience. "I'm sorry!" she said defensively. "I forgot my purse at work."

"Two seconds," he intoned in an ominous voice. "And you have to make a pledge not to spend the whole night worrying about what might be going on in your absence."

"I promise," she muttered grudgingly.

179

"I'll hold you to it," he declared. Then that sweet sexy smile claimed his features and he winked at her. "Better yet, I'll hold you to *me*."

He followed her into the house. Lynn had assured him no one was home. It was their monthly movie night. Lillian and Martha had chaperoned the five girls to the Barclay Square six-plex for Kevin Costner's latest. But he followed her anyway.

"It's in my office," she said as they stepped into the front hall. "I'll be two seconds."

"Uh-huh."

She rolled her eyes. "You're awfully suspicious for a Democrat."

"Yeah, well, we haven't been the same since that Watergate thing, you know."

Lynn chuckled and turned to head down the hall to the cram-packed disaster area that would become her office in an eon or two, but her step faltered as she drew even with the living room doorway. From the corner of her eye she caught sight of a figure on the sofa, and her heart vaulted into her throat as she whirled around.

"Who's there?" she demanded, hoping sheer terror didn't ruin the effect.

A sniffle was her only answer. She ventured inside, squinting in the gloom. The shades had been drawn and the lamps left off, leaving the room covered with heavy shadows. She automatically turned on the first table lamp she came to, illuminating a head of golden curls tucked back against the couch.

"Christine?" she asked with concern. "Honey, what's wrong? Why aren't you at the movies with everybody else?"

The girl looked up at her from where she sat on the sofa, curled into a ball of misery. Her nose and eyes were wet and drippy, and her mouth trembled. "I — I c-called my dad, like y-you said I sh-should."

Lynn sank down beside her, her heart sinking even farther. She reached out and brushed a sprig of damp curls back from Christine's cheek. She had been counseling the girl to take the first step in making amends with her father and stepmother, who had literally thrown her out into the street when she had become pregnant. Lynn had spoken with Mr. Rickman a number of times herself, trying to impart to him Christine's feelings of abandonment when he had remarried shortly after her mother's death, feelings that had driven her to seek out love from another source. Lynn had felt he was ready to talk to his daughter again, but she had intended to be present to moderate that first attempt at reconciliation, in case something went awry. Obviously, something had.

"Oh, honey," she murmured. "It didn't go very well, did it?"

Christine's eyes welled up. The next second she was in Lynn's arms, sobbing her heart out. Lynn had all she could do to keep from crying along. She'd been in Christine's shoes. She knew what it was like to be alone and pregnant. She knew the hurt of being cut off from her family and abandoned by someone she had thought loved her. She held Christine Rickman and stroked her hair and felt her own heart break all over again as Christine's pain came pouring out.

"Why does it have to be so hard?" the girl asked, her voice choked with torment.

"I don't know, sweetie," Lynn whispered, wishing with all her heart that she did. "If I had the answer to that one, I could make the world a lot better place, couldn't I?"

It was a long time before the tears were spent and they had talked everything out. Lynn listened with patience, offering sympathy and a warm hug. Finally, Christine sat back and sniffled, dabbing at her nose with the last of the tissues from the box. She looked at Lynn sideways, her mouth twisting with chagrin.

"I ruined your date." She reached out a tentative hand and touched a big wet spot on the shoulder of Lynn's silk dress. "I ruined your dress."

"Don't worry about me," Lynn said with a soft smile. Inwardly her heart gave a lurch as she remembered Erik. A glance at the clock told her her "two seconds" had stretched into an hour and a half. He would be furious with her. Well, tough spit. Christine's tears were far more important than dinner and dancing, and if he thought differently, he could just take a hike. "Believe it or not," she teased, "I've had dates before and I'll have dates again. Are you going to be all right?"

The girl shrugged, one hand rubbing her swollen belly through her oversize T-shirt.

Lynn caught the gesture and knew the uncertainty that went along with it. She gave Christine's hand a squeeze. "I'll be there when you need me, honey."

"I know. Thanks."

"Why don't you go up to bed?" Lynn suggested with a soft smile. "Using a whole box of tissues is exhausting work."

When Christine was safely upstairs and settled in bed, Lynn retrieved her purse and shut off the living room lamp. She wandered to the front door, wondering if she would have to call a cab to get home or if she should just crash on the couch here. Looking out onto the front step, she saw she would have to do neither. Erik was sitting there with his back against the stair railing, gazing up at the sky as the first stars made their appearance on the night's dark stage.

In that instant she fell in love with him. She had been teetering on the brink for days, but in that second she fell over the edge. In that instant he turned and looked up at her with all that wisdom in his eyes and the softest, warmest smile on his lips, and her heart was lost — for all the good it would do her, she thought sadly.

"Is everything all right?" he asked, his husky voice coming to her just above the sounds of the evening and the faint strains of the organ being played at St. Stephen's.

"No." She sat down on the step, her full skirt draping down to brush her feet as she wrapped her arms around her knees. She looked at him sideways and managed a smile. "But she'll make it another day.

We'll all get by and go on."

"She's got a tough row to hoe."

"Yeah, I know," Lynn said, staring out into the gathering darkness for a long moment, lost in memories. She shook off the misty haze and turned toward Erik again with a wry smile. "I figured you'd be long gone by now."

"Shows how much you know. I'm getting this date if it kills me."

"We've lost our reservation," she felt compelled to point out as Erik stood, taking her hand and drawing her up with him.

"Hey," he said with a swagger in his step as they started down the sidewalk toward his car. The crinkles beside his eyes gave him away. "*I'm* a state senator," he declared with mock arrogance. "*I've* got pull in this town. *I* can get us a table at the most exclusive place in southern Minnesota."

They dined on Colonel Sanders's finest, seated at a redwood table with a view of the stars. It was indeed exclusive. It was the only table in the house — or rather, *out* of the house. They had picked up their dinner and driven out to Erik's home in the secluded Buckthorn subdivision, where the houses were tucked back among the trees on wooded acreages. Erik's house was simple in design, a rambling tri-level structure sided in rough-sawn cedar. It blended perfectly with its surroundings, giving a sense of belonging and comfort.

"Do you like my choice of night spots?" Erik asked, his voice soft and smoky.

A slow smile curved Lynn's mouth. "Very much. The food was average, but the atmosphere doesn't leave much to be desired."

*Except you.* The words remained unspoken, but vibrated in the air between them, electric and magnetic. Their gazes caught and held and Lynn had the distinct feeling that the thought was a shared one, humming on a common wavelength, that their minds were connecting as their thoughts roused longings in them to join physically. The idea seemed almost more intimate than the act, and she pulled her gaze away from his as a delicious warmth spread through her.

She sat back against the cushions of her chair and gave herself the opportunity to appreciate her surroundings. The woods beyond the lawn were chirping with nightlife. The sky above them was a vast black bowl studded with pinpoints of diamond light. They sat on the wide deck at the back of the house with soft music floating out through the open windows. Peace was a softness in the air around them, the lack of traffic noise, the rustle of the trees.

For the first time in weeks Lynn felt herself really relaxing. She felt as if this place were a safe, secluded haven where the problems of the world couldn't touch her. *Foolishness,* that cynical voice inside her said, but for once she shushed it. She took a deep breath of the fresh night air and exhaled slowly, closing her eyes and letting her head fall back.

Erik took a sip of his wine and studied her in silence, enjoying the chance to look his fill. She sat in profile to him, her night-black hair falling in a silken cascade behind her, the slim ivory column of her throat arched. Her breasts thrust out gently, nipples budding beneath the sheer fabric of her dress.

Desire stirred deeply inside him. Tonight. Tonight he would make her his, in the oldest sense of the term. Once again the thought brought on a strong surge of some primal instinct that had lain dormant inside him. He had never thought of sex as a claiming, never viewed it as such a critical step in his relationship with a woman.

Not that he usually thought of sex in casual terms. He was a responsible man, but this was different. And the difference was Lynn. With her it would be more than just sex — it would be a surrender, an acceptance of him that went deeper than the purely physical, a letting down of that invisible barrier she protected herself with. The prospect set off a tremor inside Erik that was equal parts awe and fear.

He pushed himself slowly to his feet and held out his hand to her as he rounded the table. His gaze caught hers and drew her to him as surely as his touch. "Dance with me," he said.

Lynn went into his arms without a word, nestling her head against the hollow of his shoulder. "Unforgettable" drifted like smoke through the window screens. Erik held her close and they swayed together, shuffling in a lazy circle around the deck. A wonderful, silvery shiver went through her as he lowered his head and brushed his lips against the side of her neck. She snuggled into his embrace and tilted her head to the side, offering her throat for him to nibble and kiss. Then his mouth found hers and she sighed and melted against him.

The music might have ended or it might

have played on. Lynn ceased to be aware of it. All her senses focused on the man in her arms. He kissed her with deep, provocative strokes of his tongue, his big hands sliding down her back and pressing her closer. The scent of him filled her nostrils — warm, clean, male — awakening something basic and utterly feminine inside her. She wanted him. In a way she couldn't quite remember wanting a man ever before, she wanted Erik Gunther. The idea frightened her a little. She couldn't afford to let him get too close, couldn't afford to need him too much. But that need was swelling and throbbing inside her, demanding to be assuaged, overtaking her other emotions and swallowing them up.

"I need you, Lynn." His whisper came to her through the mists of the sensual spell that was weaving itself around them. "I want you."

"Yes," she murmured, her lips brushing the hard plane of his jaw. She kissed his cheek, kissed his throat. Sliding one hand up between them, she loosened the knot in his tie and undid the top button of his shirt. Slowly she pressed her mouth against the hollow at the V of his collarbone, kissing him deeply, caressing the tender flesh with the tip of her tongue and feeling his pulse race just beneath the surface. A deep moan rumbled up from the depths of his chest, and she felt it vibrate against her even before she heard the sound.

Erik slid his hands into her hair, sending her combs clattering to the deck and setting her mane free to fall in waves over his wrists and forearms. Tilting her head back, he looked into her face, his expression taut, intense, his eyes as bright as blue flames, burning with the heat of his desire. He lowered his mouth to hers for a kiss that was hot and urgent, and Lynn responded with equal need. She clung to him, pressed herself to him, shuddered against him as he bent her back over his arm. Then he was lifting her, carrying her.

He crossed the deck in three long strides and shouldered open the sliding glass door that led to his bedroom. The room was cast in wedges of shadow and pale moonlight, the bed a vast expanse of dark and light. Lynn took in only impressions of the room — the feel of the thick beige carpet under her stockinged feet as Erik set her down, the sense of neatness, the masculine lines of the furniture. With her attention riveted on Erik, there was no time to take in the decor or try to discern anything from it about the man who lived in this room.

He stood at the foot of the bed, his eyes locked on hers as he yanked his tie free and lifted a hand to the buttons of his shirt. Mirroring his actions, Lynn's hands lifted and settled on the top button of her dress, sliding the mother-of-pearl disk from its mooring and moving slowly down to the next one. When she reached the last button above her belt, Erik put his hands on her wrists.

"Let me," he said.

He hooked his thumbs inside the placket of the dress and slowly slid the bodice off her shoulders. Lynn attempted to raise her arms to do the same to him, but she found herself caught. As she started to try to slide one arm free of the dress, Erik stopped her again.

"Not yet," he murmured. "There's plenty of time. All night . . . forever . . ."

He lifted his hands to cup her breasts, stroking her through her sheer, silky bra. She stood perfectly still for his examination, though her breath fluttered in and out of her lungs in shallow, stuttering gasps. He kneaded and caressed, squeezed gently, relishing the size and shape of her with his fingers. Her breasts were small but plump, filling his hands perfectly. Nipples strained against the fabric of her bra, begging for his attention.

Erik slid his thumbs inside the cups and inched the fabric aside, baring her to his gaze. He was struck again by the word "beautiful," and another tremor of desire rocked through his aching body as he rubbed the pads of his thumbs across the distended peaks of her nipples.

That very same passion seared Lynn to her core. She arched into his touch and tried once more to reach for him, only to be stopped again by the silken bonds of her dress. A frustrated whimper escaped her.

"Erik, please . . ."

He dropped his mouth to hers as he helped her free herself, and groaned when her small, cool hands slid up the muscled ridges of his back. The next thing Lynn knew, the bed was beneath her and Erik was settling himself atop her, kneeing her thighs apart to fit himself intimately against her. His shirt and tie were gone, abandoned somewhere along the way. The moonlight cast him in sharp relief — silvered muscle and velvet dark shadow, light eyes and a mouth gleaming from their kisses. She stared up at him, heart racing.

"It's been a long time for me," she said quietly, not sure why she felt so compelled to tell him. It would have been better to let him think she did this kind of thing on a regular basis. It would have been better not to let him know this was special. But the need to tell him was there almost as strongly as the need to take him inside her.

Erik gazed down at her, silent for a long moment as he weighed her words and their import. "Good," he whispered at last. "I'm glad you waited for me."

"I haven't been waiting forever."

He smiled that wise little smile and shook his head, "This is the first time. *Our* first time. That's all that counts."

Lynn couldn't stop the tears that sprang up at his words. She felt so old, so battered and worn next to Erik, the white knight, the good man. And he would have her feel clean and young and pure all over again, as if the past had never happened, as if his goodness could somehow heal the sins of her youth.

*Foolishness,* the cynical voice inside her sneered. He was just a man and this would be just sex. Nothing she hadn't encountered before. But the voice couldn't stop the wave of fear that told her this *would* be something special, that once they had crossed this threshold there would be no going back.

"It's all right," Erik said softly. Tenderly, he kissed a stray tear from the outer corner of her eye. "It's *so* right, honey."

Lynn closed her eyes and surrendered herself to feeling, shutting out the doubts. She stroked her hands through Erik's hair as he kissed his way to her breast. She gasped and arched up as he took her nipple into his mouth. She concentrated on the incredible surge of sensation, the swirling, fiery rush of excitement that claimed her body. His mouth was hot and avid, drawing on her, tugging insistently, his tongue rasping gently against her sensitive point.

Then he was trailing kisses downward, in the dip between her rib cage, over her belly. Fingers fumbling, he dispensed with her belt and worked free the remaining buttons of her dress. Her panty hose presented a challenge that had him both cursing and chuckling, drawing a few giggles from Lynn as she tried to work her legs clear of the tangle. When they finally came free, Erik slingshot the hose across the room and launched himself back up on the bed, grinning as he landed beside her.

"That's what I want," he said, stroking

her hair away from her cheek as he snuggled in next to her. "To see you happy." He lowered his head and nipped at her lush lower lip, then kissed where he'd bitten. His voice dropped a husky notch as he looked her in the eyes again. "To *make* you happy."

Lynn managed a wry smile. "I think you'll have to take your pants off for that."

He complied without hesitation, tossing his slacks and shorts aside and returning to her, gloriously, unself-consciously naked. He had a beautiful body — athletic, well-proportioned, well-endowed. Lynn shivered with hunger as he settled in beside her. She couldn't stop herself from touching him. He was beautiful — sleek and male. She stroked her hands over his body, reveling in all of those aspects of him.

He lay back and allowed her the freedom to explore, quivering when she touched a ticklish spot, groaning when she lingered on a sensitive area. He sucked in a breath through his teeth when her fingers closed around his erection and she began stroking him. He was hard, hot, and pulsing in her hand, the tip of him as soft as velvet as she rubbed her thumb across it. She thought of how he would feel inside her and a tremor of need shook her.

Lynn let out a little yelp of surprise as Erik reversed their positions, tumbling her onto her back. He loomed over her, looking intense and predatory.

"My turn," he said, sliding one hand across her thigh to the delta of ebony curls that hid her most feminine secrets.

Of their own volition, her hips lifted off the bed as Erik's fingers deftly parted the swollen petals and eased into her warmth. She groaned as he tested the depth of her readiness, sliding two fingers deep while his thumb found her most sensitive flesh and brushed tantalizingly back and forth across the tiny kernel.

Lynn struggled for control of the sensations tearing through her, wanting what Erik was giving her and fighting it at the same time. Her hips bucked against his hand, but she fought to hold back from the edge he was urging her toward.

"Don't fight it, Lynn," he said in a hoarse, seductive whisper. "Let it happen."

"No."

"Come on, sweetheart, we've gone too far to stop now. Don't hold back on me, Lynn."

"Erik, please . . . please . . ." She gasped for breath, squeezing her eyes shut as she strained against release. She felt too vulnerable, too alone, exposed in a way that had nothing to do with nakedness. She didn't expect Erik to understand what she was feeling, didn't really want him to know. But he seemed to sense it. He eased his hand away from her and positioned himself between her thighs, nudging her slick, hot, woman's flesh gently as he bent his head to kiss her.

"It's all right, honey. I'll be with you. We'll go over that edge together." He kissed her again, a slow, calming kiss that gradually slid from her mouth to her jaw to her ear. "Do I need protection, honey?"

"Yes. I'm sorry."

"Hush. It's all right." Erik leaned over and rummaged through the drawer of the nightstand, telling himself he wasn't disappointed. This was the nineties, after all; women weren't inclined to go around having unprotected sex. He had always been conscientious about it himself. Still, he couldn't seem to tamp down the raw desire to bury himself in the silken heat of Lynn's body, with nothing to keep them apart, to prevent her from taking his seed. The sensation was nothing short of primitive, and it shook him a little as he tore open the foil package.

It struck him again as he slid his hands beneath her hips and lifted her for his entry. He wanted to make her *his* in the oldest, most basic way possible. He'd never felt quite this way with a woman before, and as Lynn's body closed tight and hot around him, he knew he'd never feel quite this way again.

Lynn held her breath as Erik entered her in a single slow, pushing stroke. The sensation of being invaded, of being filled, was incredible. And as she looked up at him in the pale, silvery light, the sense of joining with another human being body and soul hit her with a force that sent her reeling.

"Together," he whispered as he lowered himself to her. Clasping hands with her, he stretched her arms above her head and began to move. "Together, Lynn."

They moved in unison, their bodies in perfect harmony. Erik rocked against her, reaching deep with every thrust, nearly withdrawing only to plunge into her again. Lynn arched up to meet him, taking every inch of him and feeling every stroke all the way to her heart. She felt beyond control, beyond holding back as the passion boiled inside her, building like a head of steam. She wanted him, wanted this, and for the first time in a long time she let herself go, unable to do anything but surrender herself totally. She pulled her hands free of his and wrapped her arms around him, clinging to him as the world shattered around her and desire shattered within her.

"Erik! Oh, God, Erik!" she cried, more frightened than enraptured as wave after wave of physical ecstasy crashed over and through her.

Erik was lost in his own sea of oblivion. He slid his arms around Lynn's shoulders and clutched her to him as her body tightened around him in exquisite, mind-numbing spasms, sending him over the edge. He stiffened against her and cried out her name as he exploded within her.

# — 9 —

The fog gradually cleared from Erik's mind as his breathing slowed. He realized belatedly that he was all but crushing Lynn in his embrace, and he gradually loosened his hold, easing her back to the mattress and sliding his arms out to brace himself above her. He tenderly brushed damp tendrils of hair back from her face as he took in her expression. She looked as stunned as he felt, taken by surprise by the all-consuming power of what had just passed between them.

"It's all right, sweetheart," he whispered, his mouth curving in a gentle smile. "I love you."

He hadn't thought it was possible to fall so hard so fast, but there was no doubt in his mind. He was in love with Lynn Shaw. He knew it with absolute certainty in every cell of his being. But the shadows that came into Lynn's eyes told him she didn't share his certainty.

"You can't," she said, so softly he almost didn't hear her.

"I do."

"No."

Lynn wiggled out from under him and sat up, tugging the hunter-green bedspread across from the other side of the bed. She pulled it up around her and huddled against the smooth oak headboard, her knees drawn up to her chest, arms banded around them. In the wake of Erik's admission, her heart was pounding almost as hard now as it had been at the peak of their lovemaking.

She was caught. She had thought she would be able to get through this unscathed, untouched emotionally. She had told herself she could have this time with him because she knew better than to let her heart get involved. Who had she been kidding? She had connected with Erik the night they'd met and, despite her efforts to keep a distance, they had grown closer with each passing day and with every shared experience. Now she had joined with him physically and the heat in his eyes as he stared at her burned through her protective barriers and looked right into her soul.

*God, please don't let him see that I love him.*

Life had an exceedingly cruel sense of irony. She'd finally found a man she could love and trust, the last white knight on earth, but she couldn't allow herself to hang on to him because he was too good, too sterling. He had a record that was unblemished, a future that stretched bright and golden before him, while her past was tarnished and littered with trouble. She would ruin him. Just by touching him she would ruin him, just as she had ruined the lives of her family back in Indiana.

Erik sat on the edge of the bed watching her struggle with some terrible inner demon. Despite her efforts to fight them off, tears rose up to gleam in her eyes. She pressed a hand against her mouth and turned her face away from him, averting her gaze as if she didn't feel worthy of making that contact with him.

"Why can't I love you?" he asked gently, his look intent, taking in every nuance of her expression. She wasn't rejecting him. Not in the true sense of the word. She was retreating from him. She was afraid.

"You don't even know me," she said.

"I know all I need to know to love you. I know you're stubborn and beautiful, that you have an inner fire that lights up your eyes. I know you care about people, that you reach out to help them. You're passionate and hot-tempered and good —"

Lynn cut him off with a violent shake of

her head. Shame rose up in her throat to choke her. She couldn't sit there and listen to him extolling her virtues when she didn't have any, couldn't let him mistake penitence for goodness.

She started to move for the other side of the bed, intending to get up. Erik caught her by the arms in a grip that was gentle but unyielding. He turned her shoulders toward him, but she still refused to look at him.

"Why are you afraid to have me love you, Lynn?" he asked. "Why are you afraid to let me get that close?"

"It's too soon," she hedged, desperately wishing for a way out of this situation and fatalistically knowing there wasn't one.

"It's not," Erik insisted. "There's been something between us from the night we met. Don't try to tell me you haven't felt it too. You wouldn't have gone to bed with me if you didn't."

"How do you know that?" Lynn snapped, falling back on her old friend, belligerence. She raised her head and glared at him, ignoring the teardrop that had run down her cheek and was clinging defiantly to her chin. "You're a good-looking man, Senator. Don't try to tell me you've never had a woman want you for your body."

Anger flared in Erik's eyes. His fingers tightened on Lynn's upper arms. "Don't you dare try to tell me this is just sex. You're as tight as a virgin. You haven't been to bed with a man since there was a Democrat in the White House. You don't sleep around, Lynn, and you didn't single me out because of the way my jeans fit."

She narrowed her eyes, and another pair of tears went up and over the barrier of her lashes. "You don't know anything."

"I know I love you!" he shouted.

"How can you love me?" she shouted back. "You don't even know my name!"

Her words seemed to chill the very air around them. Everything went still. Erik stared at Lynn, his heart pounding, his mind momentarily befuddled by her words. *Didn't know her name?* It made no sense, and yet the look of horror in her eyes suggested she'd just let slip a terrible truth.

"What are you saying?" he asked, not altogether certain he wanted to hear the answer.

Lynn took advantage of his shock to pull herself free of his grasp. This time she did scramble from the bed and went in search of her clothing.

"Nothing," she murmured. Picking her

crumpled dress up from the floor, she shrugged into it and started fastening the buttons, her fingers fumbling hopelessly over the smooth mother-of-pearl disks. "Let's just say this isn't going to work and call it a night."

"Let's not." He rounded the end of the bed and caught her by the wrists. "You're telling me I went to bed with a stranger," he said, his expression fierce. "I think I deserve an explanation for that."

Lynn's facade of anger crumbled. Her shoulders sagged. She hung her head, her gaze fastening on Erik's big hands circling her wrists. The fantasy was over. She'd had her date with Prince Charming, but she hadn't made it home before midnight. The clock had struck, and now she'd turned back from a princess to . . . what? What she had been all along — a woman with a past.

Erik watched the fight go out of her, taking all his anger with it. His heart ached for her, for the pain she was putting herself through for whatever reason.

"Tell me," he whispered, sliding his arms around her and drawing her against him. He buried his face in the wild tumble of her hair and hugged her close. "You can tell me anything. You're a Russian spy. You used to be a man." He pulled back from her just enough to let her see him make a face. "Well, I guess I'd rather not hear that, but anything else I can deal with. I promise."

Lynn's heart squeezed painfully at the sweetness in his eyes. He was so good. He would try to keep his promise. But Lynn didn't hold out much hope. The understanding he had been cultivating this last week with her girls was too new and too fragile. She'd lied to him, kept things from him. The revelation of her past was bound to bring a return of Erik the Stern, Erik the Unyielding, the straight arrow who didn't tolerate bad behavior from children of "good" families.

"I'd like to dress first, if you don't mind," she said. She was going to feel naked enough with clothes on.

Erik didn't say a word. He slipped her dress from her shoulders and tossed it aside, then picked up his discarded shirt and held it for her. Lynn shrugged into it without protest, giving in to the need to at least be that close to him. She fastened the buttons while he picked up his pants and stepped into them. He seated himself on the foot of the bed, forearms braced against his thighs, hands dangling down between his knees, and waited, his gaze following her as she moved to stare out the big window.

"My name was Ellen Bradshaw," she began. "My father taught computer science at Notre Dame. My sister was brilliant. I rebelled." Such a simple story, she thought, as simple as a pebble being thrown into a pond, and with effects as far-reaching as the concentric circles of movement caused by that one small stone. "Everything Rebecca did was right, perfect, above and beyond. Dad adored her. He used Rebecca as a measure for my worth, and I always fell short because I was just ordinary. When I was little I used to knock myself out trying to please him, trying to make him proud of me, but he always had some small criticism, some way I could have done better if I'd thought about it, if I'd applied myself harder. Eventually I quit trying."

For a long moment she stared silently through the glass, seeing not the deck beyond or even her own reflection, but a dim reflection of herself at nine, in her best dress with a stain on the collar, her braid coming loose. She was standing in the doorway of their house in Mishawaka with a construction-paper turkey clutched in her hand. It was the moment she had realized with a terrible sense of clarity that her father would never love her the way he loved Rebecca, no matter what she did, no matter how hard she tried. Twenty years had passed and she could still feel that terrible hollowness in her stomach as if it had been yesterday. She pushed past it with an effort and went on.

"I told you once before I made Regan look like an honor student. That's the truth. I knew every way there was to make my father angry. It was the one thing I seemed to excel in. I cut school, I smoked dope, I drank, I stole. I hung out with the toughest, scruffiest bunch of under-achievers I could find."

The image of the nine-year-old faded and was replaced by that of a teenager who bore a sullen resemblance to Regan Mitchell — too tough to be believed, with a chip on her shoulder to rival the Rock of Gibraltar.

"Still, I managed to graduate. Deep down there was still a piece of that little girl who wanted to please Daddy, I suppose. By then he'd kicked me out of the house and I was living on the money my mother left me. I enrolled in junior college, thinking maybe I should try to straighten myself out. My father had written me off.

There wasn't anybody to play the bad girl for anymore. So I went in with good intentions, but . . . well, you know what they say about best-laid plans. . . .

"I got involved with one of my teachers. It was a classic example of seeking the love of a father figure. Of course, I was desperately sure it was the real thing. I wanted so badly for it to be. . . ." She let the words trail off as the memory of that painful longing reverberated through her like an echo. She had wanted so badly to be loved, had needed so desperately for someone to find her worthy.

"What happened?"

Erik's soft, husky voice pulled her back to the present. She pushed the old feelings aside and stated the facts simply and concisely, as if they didn't still hurt. "I got pregnant. He took a hike. Turned out he wasn't actually divorced from his wife after all. Big surprise," she said sarcastically. "He gave me two hundred dollars and told me it was over."

"Oh, God," Erik whispered. From the corner of her eye Lynn could see him rub his hands over his face in a classic male gesture of weary frustration.

"You can't *ever* begin to imagine what I felt like," she said softly, her voice trembling with the power of those remembered emotions. "I'd screwed up everything I ever touched. The one thing I hadn't done was prostitute myself, but then it turned out I'd done that, too, without even realizing it."

She could still feel it — the emptiness, the hollow feeling inside that had threatened to swallow her whole. She could still feel what it had been like to stand there in the darkened hall of the science building. She could still smell the leftover fumes lingering in the air from the chemistry lab. She could still feel those crisp green bills clutched in her fist while she watched Philip Rutger calmly stroll away from her, could still hear the dull ring of his heels against the marble floor. She hadn't been anything to him but a convenient source of sex. He'd paid her for her trouble and walked away, absolving himself of all guilt or responsibility. She'd never imagined anyone could feel as worthless and as dirty as she had felt that night. Or as alone.

Erik slipped his arms around her from behind, and Lynn wanted to cry as his warmth enveloped her. Why couldn't she have met him a lifetime ago, before she'd made her mistakes?

"What did you do?"

210

"I ran. I had the baby." She reduced those terrible months to two meager sentences, simply unable to relive them.

"You gave the baby up for adoption?"

"Oh, I went one better than that," she said with biting sarcasm. "I gave him to my sister. I believe my exact words were, 'You're so damn good at everything else, I'm sure you'll do better than me at this too.' "

Lynn closed her eyes against the pain and the fierce turmoil of emotions the memory evoked. She had never wanted anything more than she'd wanted her child, someone she could love, someone who would love her unconditionally. But she had screwed up so many times in the past. Everything she'd tried, she'd failed at miserably. She couldn't bear the thought of failing at motherhood, too, ruining her child's life just because she could never do anything right. At the same time, she had seen a way of getting revenge on her sister and of punishing her father. And so she had altered all their lives irreversibly.

"That was ten years ago," she mumbled, struck numb by the idea that she had a nine-year-old son back in Mishawaka. What would he look like by now? What would he be like? What did nine-year-old boys like to do? The knowledge that she would never find out sat as heavily as a rock in her stomach. For a long time she had punished herself by thinking of all the things she was missing out on — his first smile, his first steps, his first word. Those thoughts still hit her from time to time, and it never failed to surprise her that she had yet to run out of tears for them. They slid down her face now, unheeded, to fall onto Erik's shirt.

"A few years later," she murmured, sniffling, "I finally got myself together and started over. New name, new me, new life." After drifting and living hand-to-mouth and punishing herself in every conceivable way she could, a counselor had turned her around, believed in her, helped her, pushed her, and now she did the same for other girls. It seemed a fitting way to make restitution.

"So you see, Senator," she said on a long, sad sigh, "I'm not exactly who you thought I was."

"Aren't you?"

Erik turned her in his arms and looked down into her upturned face. She had expected him to reject her. She had expected him to stand in judgment of her life, the way he had judged Regan. He could see it in her eyes. She was waiting for the other shoe to drop, waiting for him to lower the boom. The idea made him feel ashamed of himself. How could he ever have been so pompous as to judge someone without having all the facts? It was a mistake he was determined never to repeat.

He had listened to Lynn's story, aching for the little girl who had never quite measured up, wishing with all his heart he could have been there to comfort her through the ordeal of her youth, wishing he could have been there to deal with the bastard who had left her pregnant and alone. It nearly killed him to think of her giving away her baby. He'd seen her pain, felt the raw, ragged edges of it. He would have given anything for the power to go back in time and change it all for her, to give her back her child, to give her *his* child, to hold her to him and keep her safe from all that she'd suffered.

She had certainly managed to take him down a peg or two in the short time he'd known her, he thought as he reached up to brush a stream of tears from her cheek. He'd gone from being pompous and self-righteous to taking up the sword to defend the very people he'd thought beneath him, the people who had made mistakes with their lives. Lynn had shown him how deeply the roots of those mistakes went. She'd taught him about compassion and caring and human frailty. He had no intention of letting those lessons go to waste. And he had no intention of letting this remarkable woman push him away, either.

"You're who I thought you were and then some," he said, cupping the soft, smooth curve of her cheek with his hand. "You're still the woman fighting for what she believes in. You're still the woman who'd give everything she had to help a kid in trouble. That's the woman I fell in love with."

The weariness in her eyes seemed as old as time as she looked up at him. "Don't make me out to be a saint, Erik. I'm not."

"I don't want a saint. I want you."

Lynn shook her head and backed away from him. "It can't work long-term, don't you see that?"

"I see that you're not willing to give us much of a chance."

"No, you don't see," she insisted, her voice rising with frustration. "By not getting involved with you, I *am* giving you a chance."

Her meaning hit Erik like a brick, all but knocking the wind out of him. Not only had Lynn expected him to reject her, she didn't mean to give him a choice about it. She was bowing out in the name of nobility.

"You think you're not *worthy* of me?" he said, his voice soft with disbelief, his gaze sharp with it as he searched her face for the truth. "Is that what this is all about?"

"Erik, use your head, for God's sake," she snapped, squaring her shoulders defensively. "You're a politician in a state of squeaky-clean politics. My past isn't just checkered, it's soot-black. You can't possibly believe I'd be an asset to your career."

"Pardon me," he drawled sardonically, "but it never occurred to me to fall in love with an eye toward my popularity polls."

"My luck," Lynn murmured quietly, the irony striking a poignant chord inside her. After everything else she had done wrong, she would manage to screw this up too. Knowing she would never be free of her past, she had fallen in love with a man whose bright future would depend on it.

She lowered her head in defeat and stared down at the fists she had clenched before her, as if she had literally meant to fight off Erik's love. Slowly she relaxed her hands and let them fall. The cuffs of the shirt dropped past her fingertips, making her feel small and powerless, like a little girl dressed up in her daddy's Sunday best.

"I'm so sorry," she whispered, not even sure what she was apologizing for. She had so much to regret, the words formed far too small a blanket to cover it all. Her eyes squeezed shut against the tears as pain rolled through her in waves. "So sorry," she whispered, misery choking her voice away.

She felt Erik's nearness before he touched her, sensed him so acutely that her tears came harder, driven by a kind of despair she hadn't known in ten years — the kind of despair that came from realizing she would have to give up the one thing she wanted most in the world. She wanted to clutch at Erik, to cling to him, to hold on no matter what. She knew without being told that he was the best thing that would ever happen to her, the best man she would ever know, and she could either push him away and save him or touch him and be the ruination of all his dreams.

Sobbing, she thrust her arms out, intending to fend him off. Her palms connected with the hard, hair-dusted planes of his chest and she started to bolt away, but he caught her and pulled her gently into his embrace. He wrapped his arms around her, imprisoning her trembling body against the strength of his, enfolding her in his warmth, offering her the comfort of his touch, his voice.

"We'll work it out," he said softly, his lips brushing her temple as he curled himself down over her and pulled her tighter against him. "We'll work it out."

"We can't," Lynn mumbled, her face pressed against his chest, tears running into her mouth, salty and bittersweet.

"We will," Erik insisted, as if he could force events to change with the strength of his own determination. That was the way he had been raised — to believe he could accomplish anything if he set his mind to it. He didn't want to think that this case might be the exception to the rule. He'd waited too long to fall in love to have it snatched from his grasp now. This was the woman he wanted, the woman he ached for with a need that went deeper than anything he'd ever known before. He wouldn't let her go. He wouldn't.

"I don't care who you were. I don't care what you did," he whispered urgently as he slid a hand into her hair and tipped her head back. "I love you."

He captured her mouth with his and kissed her deeply with a fervor that bordered on desperation, a desperation that intensified as he tasted Lynn's tears. The primitive need to brand her as his, to bond her to him, burned in his gut, and he swept his right hand down to the ripe curve of her buttock and lifted her against him, pressing her into his suddenly straining manhood.

Lynn felt her resolve drain away and need rise up to take its place. She didn't want to push Erik away, she wanted to hold him forever. And in that moment it didn't matter how wrong it might have been. She didn't have the strength to fight herself, didn't have the strength to be noble. All she could do was want him and need him and hope that what little she could have of him would last her a lifetime.

Instead of pushing him away, her arms slid up around his neck and she pressed herself fully against him. He kissed her over and over, deep, drugging kisses that took her mind further and further from reality, immersing her in the fantasy of belonging to him until her physical sense took complete control. She stopped thinking and simply let herself experience — the feel of his big body against her, the taste of him, the warm, masculine scent of him, the sound of his breathing, the beating of his heart. She let herself float on sensation, lost herself in the dream.

Her head fell back as Erik's mouth trailed down the column of her throat. The dress shirt slipped from her shoulders to pool at her feet. Then she was falling, being lowered to the bed, and Erik was falling with her, into her embrace, into her body. She wrapped her legs around his lean hips and welcomed him into her warmth, cherished the feel of him deep within her. She arched into his thrusts, moving with him, soaring with him into oblivion, holding at bay the sure knowledge that what their souls were sharing couldn't last.

## 10

"It's time for action when our homes are defaced and delinquents are allowed to run rampant through our neighborhoods!" Elliot Graham declared. Splashes of hectic color rose on his cheekbones. His dark eyes burned bright with the fever of righteousness as the news camera zoomed in on him. The crowd behind him gave a shout of agreement. Their signs bobbed up and down above their heads. Interspersed with the now familiar slogans were freshly printed posters that read *Graham for City Council.*

Lynn stood off to the side, watching with a sinking feeling that weighed like an anvil in her stomach. Doom was in the air. The tide of sentiment was running hard against them. Elliot Graham's followers were becoming more numerous and more vocal, and she couldn't help but think that it would be only a matter of time before the bishop silenced their roar by asking Horizon House to relocate.

They stood on Graham's back lawn, the morning sun beaming brightly across an expanse of spray-painted obscenities that decorated the entire wall of his house. Whoever was running rampant in the neighborhood, they certainly knew where to go to get the maximum reaction for their trouble, Lynn thought. In addition to the Rochester press, Elliot had managed to rouse the attentions of the Twin Cities papers, as well as the Winona *Daily News*, whose story would undoubtedly heavily influence the bishop in the growing controversy. Lynn mentally recited the words that were scrawled across the clapboard.

"I'm calling for a meeting between the mayor, the bishop, Father Bartholomew, and myself — as representative of Citizens for Family Neighborhoods," Graham said.

Lynn shook her head and tuned him out. She turned to the rest of her little knot of supporters, wanting to find some ray of hope among their faces, but there wasn't any. Father Bartholomew was wringing his hands and humming little notes of worry. As usual, his glasses were askew and his hair was disheveled, but instead of this giving him the effect of being merely unkempt, he looked frazzled, like a man who was being given electric shocks at regular intervals. Martha stood with one hand on her ample hip, a posture that suggested anger and impatience, but her other hand was rubbing insistently at the amethyst crystal she wore as a pendant around her neck — a sure sign of worry. Even Lillian, who always managed to keep her cool, who had probably looked the part of the Mayo Clinic doctor's wife since infancy, was obviously distressed. Apprehension glowed in her eyes behind her prim tortoiseshell librarian glasses and tightened her mouth into a distressed line.

"Will he get his meeting with the bishop?" Lynn asked quietly, her gaze homing in on the priest who had so valiantly come to their rescue.

Father Bartholomew huffed a little breath and pushed his glasses up on his nose. "Not for a few days, he won't, thank the angels. The bishop has gone to Chicago for a conference on the new age of miracles."

"Maybe he can bring one back for us." Lynn said dryly.

She turned toward the media spectacle just as the reporters swung their attention to Erik. He was looking stern and senatorial, a far cry from the man who had held her in his arms all night. The contrast made him seem remote, separated from her by a gap that couldn't be bridged. She cynically told herself to get used to it.

He wielded his charm like a sword to ward off Graham's accusations, striking back with a sense of conviction and compassion that managed to subdue the crowd somewhat. He restated the fact that no one had been charged with the vandalism, that people in this country were supposed to be protected by the presumption of innocence. Lynn listened, her heart swelling with love and pride as Erik demonstrated a depth she hadn't thought him capable of the first time they'd met. She listened, awed by his charisma and the power of his personality, and all she could think was that he was a man destined to go a long, long way . . . without her.

To distract herself from the hollow ache in her chest, she forced her gaze away from Erik and placed it on Elliot Graham. Anger had always been an effective defense for her against sadness, hurt, and loss, and anger was definitely what she felt when she looked at that mild-mannered engineer who had the soul of an unscrupulous evangelist. Graham had set his sights on the city council, and he was bent on using Horizon as his stepping-stone to get there. She wondered if he ever gave a thought to the lives he was affecting with his slam campaign. She wondered if he ever gave a thought to the son he was pulling along in his wake of venom.

E. J. Graham stood slightly behind his father, obviously fresh from the shower, his hair slicked into a duplicate of his father's nerdish do, his hands stuffed into the pockets of a pair of suit pants that were just a fraction too big for him. His gaze was riveted on the back of his father's head, as if he might somehow be able to reach the man telepathically if he concentrated hard enough.

Lynn's gaze narrowed as her mind picked up the thread of an idea and slowly began reeling it in. Young Graham turned away then and followed his father toward their garage as the party broke up and the crowd began to disperse.

"This isn't good, Erik." Rob William's low, clipped voice intruded on Lynn's thoughts. Erik took up a stance in front of her, blocking her view of the Graham garage. She looked up at him, her gaze locking with his. There was a private message in the depths of his blue eyes, an intimate warmth, a possessiveness, a protectiveness, an expression that resurrected the need within her. She had to fight the urge to go into his arms and lean against his strength.

"We're losing ground," the aide said, his attention darting back and forth from Erik to the retreating flock of reporters. He was a spare, wiry young man with round wire-rimmed glasses and a regimental striped tie, his sleeves rolled neatly to his elbows as if he were prepared to stick his hands into something messy — like the situation his boss was involved in. Nervous energy hummed in the air around him as he swung an arm in the direction of the graffiti. "This kind of thing doesn't go over well with the Minnesota masses, you know. If the situation deteriorates any further, we'll be at the point of having to effect some kind of damage control, image-wise."

Erik shot his employee a piercing look. "I'm not in this for the sake of my image, Rob," he said, his voice as sharp as the crack of a whip.

The aide flinched a bit in response, his eyes rounding. He came to heel like a repentant bird dog, visibly stepping back over the line he'd crossed. "Of course not, Senator."

"I've got a call in to Judge Gunderson. Get back to his office and see if we can set something up for later today."

"Yes, sir." William ducked his head deferentially and trotted off to see to his boss's orders.

Erik held Lynn's gaze for a moment, obviously weighing his choice of words. At last he said, "This is not good, Lynn."

Lynn bridled at the subtle implication that it was the fault of one of her girls and therefore her fault. "Well, don't look at me, Senator," she said tightly. "I have an alibi for last night."

His cheeks colored slightly, but he didn't back down. "Can all your girls say that?"

No, and he knew it. Lynn's jaw tightened. Her hands curled into fists at her sides. Martha and Lillian had greeted her that morning with the news that Regan had managed to ditch them at the movies and had come sneaking back into the house at two in the morning. The girl had had plenty of time to do the deed, and God knew it wasn't beyond her, but Lynn just couldn't let herself believe Regan was guilty.

"If Regan is the one doing this, then Horizon will have to take responsibility," Erik said gravely. "You can't just go on hoping she isn't the problem and let her shenanigans ruin everything for the home and the rest of the girls."

"Erik is right," Lillian said, stepping forward, hands folded primly against her flowered voile skirt, her expression both earnest and apologetic. "We've given her so many chances, Lynn, and she isn't showing any sign of coming around. If she's not only resisting us but trying to get us shut down besides, we'll have to send her home."

Lynn looked from Lillian to Martha. Lillian was all rules and regulations. Martha was the one who went on instinct. Martha was the one who could always see past a show of bravado. Martha was meeting her gaze with a look of regret.

"We can't sacrifice everything we've worked so hard for, Lynn," she said gently. "It might be time to effect some damage control of our own."

Lynn stepped back from them, feeling hurt and betrayed, as if she were the one they were accusing of painting swearwords on the side of Elliot Graham's house. Sometimes they lost one. She knew that. She just didn't want Regan to be one of those negative statistics in their books.

"Why didn't anybody catch her at it?" she challenged, planting her hands at the waist of her jeans and tilting her chin up to a pugnacious angle. "Elliot Graham has the cops combing this neighborhood every night. Why didn't they catch her?"

Her only answer was silence. The group stood regarding her intently, their brows furrowed in thought.

"If Regan was that bent on causing trouble for Horizon, don't you think she'd *want* to get caught — the same way she always wanted to get caught shoplifting and smoking dope, so she could humiliate her parents?"

"Maybe she's tired of seeing juvenile hall," Erik offered.

"And maybe she isn't guilty," Lynn countered.

"You see too much of yourself in her, Lynn," he murmured.

The rest of the group ceased to exist for Lynn in that moment. She and Erik had moved to a different plane of understanding. He had listened to her story. He had believed her. He had offered her comfort and caring. She had watched him grow over the course of their relationship, had watched him struggle to become more understanding. If she could get him to go this one extra step, at least she would feel she'd given him something worthwhile when the time came to let him go.

She looked up at him with her heart in her eyes, begging him to take that step with her. "If *you* could see a little bit of me in her, too, Erik, you might give her the benefit of the doubt."

Erik took a slow, deep breath of morning air, his eyes steady on Lynn's. This was a test. She'd given him his chance to prove himself to her; now she was going to put his character to the test to see just how sincere he was. He could see the trap as plain as day, but there was nothing for him to do but step into it. He had made his decision. He would accept any challenge, pick up any gauntlet, if it meant winning his lady's heart.

"I hope you have a plan here, Ms. Shaw," he said.

The smile that beamed across her face was worth whatever damage this situation might do to his career, he thought with a wry smile for the image-conscious man he had been a scant few days ago. Love was leading him down a dangerous path, especially considering that the lady holding his hand had every intention of leaving him in the dust. But as with every struggle he'd ever faced, he planned to come out of this a winner — with his heart intact and Lynn Shaw by his side.

"This is a lot more exciting on television," Lynn remarked, hunkering down in her seat.

She placed her left ankle over her right knee and crossed her arms, resettling herself for what she knew could be a long and fruitless wait. She had left the house with Erik a little after eight-thirty, making it known to one and all that they were going to a late movie, but they had only driven around the corner, where they had parked Erik's Thunderbird and left it. They were ensconced now in a musty, dusty '69 Ford Fairlane that Father Bartholomew stored in the garage behind Horizon House. The car afforded them a clear view of the back door. If and when Regan left the house, they would follow her as best they could on foot.

They'd been waiting nearly two hours. The neighborhood was cloaked in darkness and quiet. Even on a Saturday night, this was not an active part of town. The grills had been cooled down and put away, the lawn chairs folded. Everyone had gone indoors to escape the mosquitoes and watch television or turn in early after a long, hard day of lawn maintenance. The last of the interior lights went off at St. Stephen's, leaving glowing only the enormous lantern that hung on a chain above the main entrance. In the dark the building looked more like a medieval castle than ever, its stone turrets rising up against the night sky.

Father Bartholomew emerged from the side door, fumbling with his keys and trying to keep a pair of books tucked under his arm. The books slipped to the sidewalk with a thump. As he bent to retrieve them, his glasses fell off, then he dropped the keys. "Well, fiddlesticks," he grumbled, his voice carrying plainly across the expanse of lawns. He gathered himself and his things together and trundled off toward the rectory, the shadows of the buildings swallowing him up in darkness.

As his footsteps faded away, Erik turned to Lynn, the corners of his mouth turning up. "We could make it more exciting," he said, his smoky voice low and suggestive as he slid an arm around her shoulders.

"Some cop you would have made," she jeered, elbowing him playfully in the ribs. "Making out on stakeouts while crime runs rampant in the streets. Do you think that's how Reuter and Briggs spend their shift?"

"God, I hope not," Erik said with feeling.

He settled his arm around Lynn's

shoulder and eased her against his side. She offered no protest, though she thought it probably would have been best for both of them if she had simply moved away. She didn't have the heart to do it, not tonight, not when so much was still hanging in the balance. She didn't want to feel alone tonight. She didn't want to feel alone any sooner than was absolutely necessary.

Funny, she thought as she stared at the little plastic statue of the Virgin Mary that was glued to the dashboard, she'd been alone for so long the feeling had just become a part of her. It had been absorbed into who she was: She had black hair and green eyes, she had a bad temper, and she was alone. She had ceased to think of it as an affliction. Until now. It had been so long since she had wanted something more than the life she'd carved out for herself, she'd forgotten what it was to yearn for something beyond her reach.

She leaned her head against Erik's chest and closed her eyes against the pain welling in her chest. She had Horizon — at least for the moment. She had her girls. She had Lillian and Martha. That was all she was allowed, and she felt damn lucky to have them after the mess she'd made of her early life. She wasn't allowed to want more. She sure as hell wasn't allowed to want this knight in shining armor sitting with his arms around her. But she couldn't let go of him just yet.

Tipping her head back, Lynn sought Erik's mouth with her own, hungrily, kissing him with all the urgency of the turmoil that swirled inside her. Twisting around on the seat of the Fairlane, she sought to press herself against him, wishing she could just become part of him, a part he could keep and cherish.

"Hey," he whispered, feathering kisses along her jawline. "It's all right, sweetheart. We'll work everything out. We will," he insisted, stroking a hand over her hair.

Lynn settled back in her place, embarrassed at the way she had allowed her emotions to break through the surface of her control. She pulled her feet up on the seat, raising a minor cloud of dust, and wrapped her arms around her knees to keep herself from touching Erik again.

"Just thought I'd sneak a quick one before the action starts," she said, hoping he wouldn't call her on her feeble attempt at lightening the situation. She glanced at him out of the corner of her eye. He was watching her, quietly considering. She hadn't fooled him, but he let it slide, and

Lynn had all she could do to keep from exhaling a sigh of relief. The confrontation would come, of that she had no doubt, but at least it wouldn't come now.

"There may not *be* any action, you know," he said, relaxing back against the seat. He rested one hand on the steering wheel and stared out the windshield at the towering walls of St. Stephen's. "Graham has put a lot of pressure on the police department to patrol the neighborhood at regular intervals. Anyone trying something tonight would just be asking for trouble."

"Asking for *something*," Lynn said.

"You really think Graham's son is behind this, don't you?"

"I'm willing to bet he is. He's trying so hard to be like his father it almost hurts to watch. Elliot is too wrapped up in his cause to notice. He treats E.J. like a secretary instead of a son."

"You think the boy is committing the vandalism to win his father's attention."

"Or to help win his father's campaign for him by 'proving him right,' so to speak. If he can make everyone believe the Horizon residents are as much a detriment to the neighborhood as Elliot has portrayed them to be, then he'll help his father win that city council seat. It's a classic case of a

234

child seeking parental approval. They don't always make the best choices as to how to go about it. Believe me, I know."

"But even if Graham's son is the one responsible, that doesn't solve the mystery of Regan's clandestine journeys."

"No, it doesn't."

Lynn's shoulders sagged a little under the burden of that particular weight. She'd had another heart-to-heart with Regan that morning, with nothing to show for it but frustration. Regan had wedged herself into the corner of her bed, her back against the wall, and locked herself up inside a shell of hostility and distrust.

*"Why should I tell you anything? You'll only come down on me for breaking all your freaking rules. You're not on my side, so just cut the 'I'm your best friend' routine."*

*"Right now I am your best friend, Regan. In fact, I'm about the only friend you've got."*

*"Bull. You're my freaking jail keeper. I'm not telling you anything, and if that screws up your plans for your precious Horizon House that's just too damn bad."*

"I'm afraid I'm going to lose her no matter what," Lynn murmured, admitting her fear aloud for the first time. "I want so badly to help her, but I just can't seem to reach her."

Erik listened to the pain and the bewilderment in Lynn's voice, and he held her hand to offer what comfort he could. She seemed so genuinely puzzled by her inability to get through to Regan Mitchell. It seemed as if she were standing in front of a mirror trying to reach through it to touch her own reflection.

"Could anyone have reached *you* at that age?" he ventured softly.

"I don't know," she whispered, staring unseeing through the dirty windshield of the car. "No one really tried."

The sadness in those words went straight to Erik's heart and stuck there, as sharp and piercing as needles. He looked at Lynn and tried to picture her young and pregnant and alone, and anger burned inside him, anger toward the people who had meant so much to her who had turned her away, and anger toward himself. He wanted to think he would have protected her, defended her, been a father to her child, but the truth of the matter was he probably would have been at the head of the line to ridicule her. What a pompous, self-righteous hypocrite he was. And Lynn thought *she* wasn't worthy of *him*.

"I love you," he said, needing her to hear it. It couldn't change what had happened in her past, but somewhere in his heart he believed it could change their future. The words might bind her to him, might hold her close, might be the one thread that would keep her from breaking away. If she knew he loved her, *really* loved her . . . He wanted to have a chance with her, a chance to slay dragons for her and right wrongs and live up to the image she had of him.

"Erik, please don't —"

He silenced her with a finger to her lips. His gaze locked on hers in the faint light. "Don't tell me not to love you, Lynn. Don't."

He lowered his head, intending to silence any protest with his kiss, but a movement at the back of the house caught his eye and he jerked his head around, searching the shadows, willing his eyes to see past the darkness.

"It's Regan," he whispered. "I'd know those combat boots anywhere."

Lynn slipped farther down on the seat of the Fairlane until she was kneeling on the floor and peering over the dash. Regan had climbed out of the second-floor bathroom window and was making her way carefully down the sloping roof of the bay window directly below it. For an instant she was caught in a wedge of streetlight that illuminated her pale skin and dark clothing. Then she was in shadow again as she dropped down onto the lawn.

She came straight toward them, and for one terrible moment Lynn thought the girl might have been using the tumbledown old garage as a hiding place, that she would walk right in and find them there waiting for her like hunters lying in wait for some unsuspecting doe. But she ducked away at the last second, skimming her fingernails down the side of the building as she made her way past it to the alley.

Lynn let out a breath and an expletive. "I never would have made it as a spy."

"Too late now, Mata Hari," Erik said, easing open the driver's door.

They skulked down the alley like a pair of thieves, keeping to the cover of a row of overgrown lilac bushes that grew behind St. Stephen's rectory. Erik led the way, towing Lynn along behind him like a recalcitrant child. Lynn lagged back, terrified of having Regan hear them.

If the girl caught her at this game of hide-and-seek, that would be the end of Lynn's chances with her. Lynn knew the one thing that would absolutely destroy all hope would be a breach of trust, and Regan would definitely see being followed as that. It wouldn't matter that Regan didn't deserve to be trusted. Therein lay the challenge. Lynn remembered it well — anyone wanting to reach her would have to want to do it in spite of all the rotten things she did. Regan wouldn't see this for what it was — Lynn trying to prove the girl's innocence. She would see it as just the opposite — Lynn trying to prove her guilt, trying to catch her at something.

They crossed the street, ducking behind parked cars as Regan hurried on ahead, almost breaking into a jog at points. Wherever she was going, she was eager to get there. She stepped around the corner of a house, disappearing just as a police cruiser turned the corner onto a side street. Erik pulled Lynn behind a privet hedge and they crouched down holding their breath as the car slowed, then moved on by. That was all they needed, she thought, to get caught sneaking through people's lawns in the dead of night. The headlines flashed before her eyes.

"Which way did she go?" Erik whispered.

Lynn snapped back to the present. "I'm not sure. Listen, Erik, maybe this wasn't such a good idea. If someone catches us, your reputation —"

"Will you let *me* worry about my reputation?"

"But —"

"Come on. I see her."

He didn't give Lynn the chance to refuse. He turned and moved, dragging her along in his wake like a rag doll. Her sneakers scuffed on the cement of the driveway as Erik led her after their quarry. They crossed another street and doubled back to the north, hurrying to keep Regan in sight, struggling to keep quiet and keep hidden. Lynn's lungs burned as she tried to keep from panting aloud for breath. She got a stitch in her side from running bent over. And all the while, an awful sense of foreboding was building in her gut. She didn't want to know the outcome of this journey, because instinctively she knew it was going to be bad. It wasn't the knowledge of guilt — it was intuition, a sense of déjà vu, a heaviness in the air. She wanted to turn around and run, but there was nowhere to run to and no time, because just as she was gathering the strength to stop and turn, Erik dropped to his knees behind a Dumpster and jerked her down with him.

Lynn glanced around her, taking a reading on their location. They'd gone maybe five or six blocks toward downtown, reaching the outer fringe of the business district, where low-rent houses intermingled with fix-it shops and auto-parts stores. The Dumpster they were crouched behind sat in back of one of the cinder-block buildings, at the back of a weedy patch of dirt that had been cleared away for employee parking. The security light above the back door of the business was broken, but enough light drifted from the streetlamp on the corner to make visibility relatively good.

Regan stood leaning against the building, smoking a cigarette, nervously tapping the toe of her boot. She choked a little on the smoke, swore under her breath, and tossed the cigarette away as she pushed herself from the wall and started pacing. She was obviously waiting for someone. Possibilities ran through Lynn's mind at a frantic pace. It was the kind of spot a kid might meet a pusher. Regan had gotten into trouble with drugs before. Lynn hadn't seen any signs of abuse in the girl since she'd come to Horizon, but that didn't mean she wasn't ready to start again. Maybe she'd been biding her time. Maybe she'd had trouble making a connection with the right person.

Maybe she was here for a different reason altogether.

The terrible sense of foreboding, the foreshadowing of coming doom swelled up inside Lynn and crystallized into a cold, hard, jagged rock in her chest as a second person dressed in dark clothing skipped around the side of the building and Regan went immediately into his arms.

Elliot Graham Junior.

## 11

*Sluts.*

The word sliced through Lynn like a knife as she watched E. J. Graham groping Regan. There was something more than youthful urgency in his movements as he kissed her and ran his hands up and down her body. Anger came to Lynn, and she recalled with a shiver the venom in his voice that first night on the lawn of the house as he'd filled in the blank of his father's statement about "their kind." *Sluts.*

"Oh, God," she whispered.

Tears rose up to blur the scene before her and Lynn lifted her hands to press them against her mouth. This was no young lovers' tryst. This wasn't E. J. Graham rebelling against his father's right-wing rule. It was no modern-day version of Romeo and Juliet. This was cruelty. Cruelty of one of the worst kinds. E. J. Graham was taking gross advantage of a lost, vulnerable girl. He was using her and cloaking that use in the guise of the one thing Regan Mitchell needed and craved above all else — love.

Erik must have sensed the malevolence, too, because his hand tightened on Lynn's and he growled the word "bastard" under his breath. He crouched beside her, his big body tense, his gaze riveted on the tableau being played out before them in the parking lot of Schultz Plumbing and Heating.

The physical activity had begun to take on a more frantic edge. Graham backed Regan up against the side of the building, his hands fumbling to tug out the hem of the black tank top she wore tucked in her jeans, his movements rough and insistent. Regan squirmed and shoved at him. When she spoke her voice was missing the sharpness, the toughness that had characterized every conversation she'd ever had with Lynn. She sounded exactly like what she was: young and confused and a little bit afraid, not nearly as hardened as she liked to pretend she was.

"E.J., stop it! You're going too fast."

"You said tonight, Regan," he snapped impatiently. "Come on."

"But not here —"

"What difference does it make?"

A little sob caught in the girl's throat as she shoved him again. "It matters. Don't say it doesn't. I want it to be nice. I thought you did too. E.J., please —"

Graham gave her a shake as he spat out a virulent curse. "You said you'd come across tonight and you'd damn well better, you little whore."

Regan cried out and tried to jerk away from him. He grabbed her arm with one hand and hauled back the other as if he had every intention of striking her.

Lynn bolted away from the Dumpster, a shout of outrage tearing from her throat, but Erik was a step ahead of her. Fury surging through him, he was across the parking lot in four long, loping strides. He grabbed E. J. Graham by the scruff of the neck, jerked the boy away from Regan, then gave him a rough shove that sent him sprawling on his hands and knees in the dirt and gravel.

There were a dozen things Erik wanted to say as he stood glaring down at Elliot Graham Jr., but his usual eloquence deserted him as his anger rose up and formed a logjam in his chest and throat. He looked down at the "good" young citizen, the son of the man who was so vocally, so piously preaching for safe, morally upstanding neighborhoods, and shook his head in disgust.

"You make me sick," he growled. "You

and your father both. Get out of here."
Graham cowered at his feet, cringing like a
whipped dog, whimpering and sniveling.
Erik lunged at him, his voice booming like
thunder in the night. "Get out of here!"

The boy scrambled away, slipping and
stumbling as he gained his feet and ran
from the lot. Somewhere down the block a
dog let loose a short cannonade of barks,
then the only sound was a soft, miserable
crying. Erik turned to see Regan standing
with her arms banded across her stomach
as if she were in physical pain. Even in the
dim light he could make out the expression
of torment on the girl's face, and for the
first time since he'd met her Erik's heart
went out to her. She was Lynn, young and
alone, caught up in the snare of her own
mistakes and abandoned by the one person
she had allowed herself to trust. Compassion swelled inside Erik in an aching tide.

"Did he hurt you?" he asked, knowing
what a stupid question it was. Of course
she was hurt. She was hurt in a way no
doctor could heal. Hurt and humiliated.
He cursed E. J. Graham, and he cursed his
inability to exact justice. If the law had allowed it, he would have kicked young Graham's butt to St. Paul and back. As it
stood, he had prevented the crime. The

court would find the boy guilty of nothing more than a case of raging hormones and poor judgment. Breaking a fragile young heart wasn't against the law.

Regan didn't answer. She looked down at the ground, hiccuping and choking on the tears she was trying so hard to hold back.

"Come on, honey," Lynn said softly. "Let's go home."

She reached out to take the girl by the arm, but Regan jerked away from her. The rejection cut Lynn like a knife. She wanted to comfort, to mother, to soothe her own remembered pain by trying to soothe Regan's, but Regan wasn't going to allow it. Forcing her chin up to a proud angle, the girl walked away, leaving Lynn with nothing to do but fall in step behind her.

It was a long walk home. Lynn felt as if she were trooping along on one of history's infamous death marches — the Trail of Tears, Bataan. She wanted to reach out to help the girl in front of her, but she couldn't, and she had to face the fact that she might never get the chance. Regan might never forgive her for following her or for witnessing her humiliation at the hands of E. J. Graham. She tried to content herself with the knowledge that she and Erik might well have prevented a rape. She doubted Regan would have come forward had no one been there to stop Graham. Regan would have kept her own counsel, never trusting anyone to believe her story. Why would anyone believe her? She was one of "those girls" from Horizon House and E. J. Graham was the son of a man running for city council on a morality platform.

All the pain Lynn felt on Regan's behalf concentrated itself into a burning knot just above her right eye. She lifted a hand to rub it wearily, barely finding the strength to plant one foot in front of the other. She wanted nothing more than to lie down, curl into a ball, and shut the world out. Then Erik slipped his arm around her shoulders and gave her a squeeze, and she amended her wish. She wanted nothing more than to lie down with Erik and shut the world out, to lose herself in the comfort of those strong arms, to cleanse herself in his goodness.

They turned in at the alley that ran behind St. Stephen's, following the same path they'd taken out. Regan trudged ahead, like a queen going to her execution, head held high, shoulders rigid. She turned to duck through a gap in the lilac hedge and came up short so quickly, Lynn almost plowed into her.

"Regan, what —" The rest of the question vaporized as Lynn followed the girl's shocked gaze.

A dark figure crouched in the shadows along the towering limestone wall of St. Stephen's. An ominous hissing sound cut through the quiet of the night. The sound of a snake poised to strike — or a can of spray paint at work.

"Wait here," Erik ordered. He gave Lynn's shoulder a squeeze and was gone, running silently back along the hedgerow and disappearing around the corner.

Lynn squinted into the darkness, trying to make out features, gender, anything that might give a clue to the identity of the person defacing the side of the church, but it was too dark, the perpetrator too far away and too well disguised, clad in black virtually from head to toe. It might have been a man or a woman, a teenager or someone older. There was simply no way to tell. Whoever it was, he or she gave the paint can one last shake, then tossed it aside.

Lynn grabbed Regan's wrist in a death grip and leaned close to the girl, never taking her eyes off the dark figure that turned and moved silently to the side door of the church and slipped inside.

"Regan, take my keys. Go into the house and call nine-one-one. Tell them someone is breaking into St. Stephen's. Hurry!"

Regan broke for the house at a run. Lynn made a beeline for the church and the door the vandal had gone through with such ease of familiarity. Heart pounding, pulse roaring in her ears, the sickeningly sweet scent of spray paint filling her nostrils, she dashed into the shadows along the side of the building and pulled up at the door. Her hand stilled on the knob as she tried to form some kind of a plan.

The vandal was inside — vandalizing, she supposed. Probably armed. Most likely dangerous. She didn't know where Erik was. He had presumably gone around to the front of the church with the intent of catching the culprit in a squeeze play, but if he didn't know the vandal had slipped into the church . . .

Lynn gave herself a mental shake. There wasn't time for theories or game plans. There was only time for action. She had always been one to act first and think later, anyway. With the thought of vindicating her girls uppermost in her mind, she turned the knob on the door and pulled it toward her.

In the next instant a dozen things seemed to happen at once. Her mind captured the flurry in quick freeze-frame shots — a black-clad figure rushing toward her, Erik coming hard behind him, a crucifix slashing down through the air at her. Erik shouted her name, yelled for her to look out, but there was no time to react.

The crucifix hit her with a glancing blow on the side of her head and she staggered backward. Her assailant lunged at her, trying desperately to shove her aside, but she grabbed his arm and held on — out of reflex to catch herself and out of instinct to catch him. He barreled through the door, threw himself against her, then veered hard away from her, breaking her hold. He stumbled off the edge of the step and Lynn hurled herself after him, flinging herself hard against his back. They went down in a teeth-jarring tumble and she had the satisfaction of hearing him grunt as his breath left him, but he threw her off and scrambled to his feet.

He hadn't gone two steps when Erik came flying through the door and off the step. The pair went down with a thud and a groan.

Lynn pushed herself to her knees, panting, and swiped a tangle of hair out of her eyes. At the same moment, Erik sat up, digging a knee into the back of the culprit to hold him in place, facedown on the turf. He shot her a look that was both fierce and triumphant, reminding her of his Viking ancestors.

"Would you care to do the honors of unmasking this piece of dirt?" he asked.

Lynn scrambled forward. "With pleasure."

Car doors banged in the distance. The back porch light at Horizon went on. Lynn could hear the sounds of people hurrying across the lawn, but her attention was riveted on the person Erik had pinned to the lawn. She reached for the edge of the ski mask, jerked it off with one motion, and her heart stopped.

Elliot Graham glared up at her, his zealot's eyes burning bright with fury.

"I don't want to talk to you."

Lynn stepped into the bedroom and closed the door behind her, ignoring what Regan claimed her wishes were. It was almost 1:00 a.m. She had endured the seemingly endless questions from the police, from Father Bartholomew, from Martha and Lillian, and from the girls, who had all been roused out of bed by the commotion. She was tired. Her head was throbbing. A goose egg had raised up where Graham had hit her with the stolen crucifix. She wanted very much to go home and soak in a nice hot bath, to soothe the aches and pains she had accumulated during the tussle, but she wasn't going anywhere just yet.

Regan sat on the edge of her bed, staring out the window that overlooked the backyard. She had claimed this room for herself the first night. It was farthest away from everyone and too small for more than one bed. A quiet, safe haven she could cocoon herself in . . . or a cell where she could sentence herself to solitary confinement. Probably the latter, Lynn thought, glancing around at the bare white walls. Regan had done nothing to make this her home. She had brought no personal things with her, no boom box, no stuffed animals, none of the usual fripperies of the teenage girl. There were no posters of rock stars on the walls, no fashion magazines scattered on the floor. There was nothing but a cheap old white-and-gold French provincial-style bedroom set and a white hobnail glass lamp with a frilly pink shade.

The loneliness of the room closed in on Lynn, the sense of self-exile drawing out deeply rooted memories like slivers that pricked and stung her heart again. Regan had tried to insulate herself with loneliness, but the ploy hadn't worked. Instead, it had driven her to reach out to E. J. Graham to ease her sense of isolation.

"He was using me," she said, the resignation in her voice overshadowing the bitterness. "I guess I should have known he was a jerk."

"It's not always that easy to tell," Lynn murmured. She sank down on the very edge of the bed, giving Regan her space, and sat bent over with her forearms on her thighs. There were grass stains and dirt on Lynn's jeans. She picked at one of the spots, wincing as she hit a bruise that was hidden beneath the denim. "I'm sure no one would have guessed his father was as much of a creep as he turned out to be either."

"Like father, like son," Regan grumbled.

"Elliot had been indoctrinating him for a long time. It's hard enough for kids to make the right choices in the best of circumstances, let alone when someone is hitting them over the head with a lot of propaganda."

Regan jerked her head around, making eye contact for the first time since Lynn had entered the room. Her eyes were red-rimmed from crying, black-rimmed from mascara that hadn't held up under the onslaught of tears, and burning with blue fire. "Are you making excuses for him?"

Lynn shook her head. "No, honey, I most certainly am not. Nothing could excuse the way he treated you. I'm just trying to understand him a little better," she said calmly. "How are you feeling?"

Regan looked away quickly, swiping at her nose with the back of her hand. "What's the difference? You want to be able to send me back to my folks with a clear conscience and a clean bill of health?"

"I'm not sending you anywhere."

"Yeah, right. That's why you were following me tonight — so you could catch me at something and have a good reason to get rid of me."

"I'm sorry we had to follow you, Regan, but there was no other way to prove you weren't behind the vandalism."

"They would have pinned it on me, wouldn't they? E.J. would have lied about meeting me. I would have been without an alibi." She had a lawyer's mind, Lynn thought, wondering how long it would take for Regan to see how bright she was, how bright her future could be. Longer than this night, that was for certain.

"Of course everyone would have believed I did it," Regan said bitingly, raising her hands in surrender. Her mouth twisted in a parody of a smile. Tears rose in her eyes and clogged her throat, leaving her hoarse. "Anyone can see I'm just rotten to the core. Good for nothing — except maybe a little fun out behind the old plumbing shop."

She pressed a hand against her mouth and fought the tide of hurt and despair so hard her face turned red. Lynn shifted positions subtly, edging a little closer.

"I see something a lot different than that when I look at you, Regan," she said softly. "I see someone good caught up in a lot of bad stuff. I know what that's like. You get into it a little at a time and pretty soon you're in so deep you're not sure how to get back out — or even if you deserve to. I've been there, honey. I know how much it hurts. I know how scary it can be."

Regan was trembling visibly now, fighting to hold herself together, shaking as she choked back a sob. Lynn's heart went out to her, but she held her position, knotting her fists into the pink chenille bed-spread to keep from moving too soon. The girl shuddered, caught in the grip of an agony Lynn remembered well. She gasped for breath, rocking herself on the edge of the bed, her hands gripping her upper arms so hard her fingers lost all color.

"H-how d-did you g-g-get out?" she stuttered.

Lynn closed her eyes for an instant and offered a quick prayer of thanks. "Someone held out a hand," she said. "And every time I batted it away, she held it out again. Finally, when I was sure she wasn't just going to yank it away, I grabbed it and hung on."

Slowly she turned toward Regan and stretched out a hand. The girl looked at it, her eyes brimming with tears and fear. Then she looked past it to Lynn and the dam burst. The barriers crumbled, the tears gushed forth, and Regan went into her arms, crying for help and begging for forgiveness. And Lynn just hung on.

Erik was waiting for her when Lynn finally descended the stairs. He was sitting in one of the overstuffed chairs in the living room, his head back, his big, sneakered feet up on the coffee table. The

257

lamp on the end table cast a wash of buttery light over him, softening the lines of weariness that were etched beside his eyes and mouth.

He looked up at Lynn as she walked in, and smiled that warm, wise smile that made her heart turn over in her chest. A small knot of anxiety stirred in her stomach. She had become much too attached to that smile. The idea of never seeing it again was getting difficult to face. She pushed the thought aside, too tired to deal with it. It had been a long night. She simply didn't have the strength left to do the right thing.

"I thought you'd be home by now, getting your beauty sleep," she said quietly.

"Shows how much you know." Erik hauled himself up out of the chair, and stretched. He'd had no intention of leaving without Lynn in tow. He knew the way her mind worked. She would see catching Graham and putting an end to the controversy over Horizon House as a natural place to end their relationship. *Think again, sweetheart.*

"Yeah. I guess I'm not as smart as I thought I was," she said, her brow furrowing. "I never would have suspected Elliot."

"That just shows you're a failure as a cynic. There's hope for you after all."

Lynn shook her head in disbelief as she thought of the man who had so piously preached about the dangers of letting "girls like those" into a nice family neighborhood. "He didn't even seem sorry for what he'd done, just angry that we caught him doing it."

"I imagine he excused it all in the name of a good cause. He thought he was hastening the inevitable by doing the vandalism himself."

"Hastening himself onto the city council so he could fight for the greater good of Rochester," Lynn said bitterly. "The end justifies the means."

Erik slid his hands along her shoulders, kneading the rigid muscles, trying to get her to let go a little of the tension. She was like a lioness defending her cubs whenever anyone threatened Horizon or her girls. They were her family, he realized, taking the place of the child she had given up and the father and sister she had left behind.

Her shoulders started to sag grudgingly under the tender ministrations of his fingers. She sighed and let her head fall back, her lashes drifting down like delicate black snowflakes against the ivory of her cheeks.

*I'd give you a family, Lynn,* he thought, the need to shelter and nurture rising up inside him like a flame.

"Well, it's over now," he murmured. "How's Regan?"

"Hurting."

It was Erik's turn to shake his head in disbelief, both at young Graham's actions and at the power of the fury that had roared through him in that parking lot. He had been raised to treat women with respect and he thought little of men who didn't hold to that rule, but what he'd felt in that instant had been magnified a hundred times by his feelings for Lynn and by thoughts of her being in Regan's place.

"You'll never know how close I came to punching that kid in the mouth," he said.

A bittersweet smile turned the corners of Lynn's mouth. She slipped her arms around his lean waist and hugged him. "Our white knight, charging to the rescue."

Erik brushed off her glowing description of him. "I'm not nearly as chivalrous as you make me out to be. I thought Regan was guilty as sin. I only went along with you because I wanted to score a few points in my favor."

And to be there for her if things went

badly, Lynn thought, to protect her and support her. He was every bit as good as she made him out to be. That little ball of anxiety rolled around in her stomach like a marble, cold and hard, and she squeezed her arms tighter around Erik. "Consider them scored," she said.

Erik stroked a hand over her hair and pressed a kiss to the top of her head. "Come home with me tonight."

Lynn pressed her cheek against his chest and listened to his heartbeat for a long moment. She shouldn't. It probably would be easier on them both if she simply said no and thus begin the process of breaking it off with him. But she couldn't say the word. She was so tired, physically and emotionally. Tired of being alone. It was late. In the morning there would be the press to deal with. They would hail Erik as the conquering hero and drag him off for interviews. They would lead him away from her and back to the world he was used to dealing with, the world he was destined for. And she would let them. But not tonight. He could be hers for a few more hours tonight.

"Yes," she whispered.

They made love slowly, tenderly, savoring every touch, every kiss. Lynn absorbed everything about the experience, recording it in her mind and in her heart like a piece of videotape to be replayed again and again when this time was over. Every detail of the room registered — the shade of tan on the walls, the plushness of the carpet, the glow of the light on the lamp's brass base, the dull sheen of the finish on the fine oak furniture. She memorized the smell of the room — sandalwood and the scent of the trees drifting in on a cool breeze through the open glass door. Her senses seemed heightened, hypersensitive, overreacting to every stimulus. The rustle of the sheets seemed louder, the musky scent of lovemaking was like a heavy perfume in the air, the slightest touch of Erik's hand against her skin made her breath catch.

"Does that hurt?" he asked.

Lynn blinked up at him, belatedly realizing she'd moaned aloud as his fingertips had traced the line of her shoulder.

"There's a bruise," he pointed out, drawing a careful circle around a darkening spot the size of a fifty-cent piece.

"I've got more than one," she said with a wry smile. "Now I know how the tackling dummy feels after football practice."

A rush of anger burned through Erik at the idea of his lady being hurt. The emotion didn't shake him quite as much as it had the first few times. He was in love, *really* in love for the first time in his life, and he suspected it would be the only time, that Lynn was the one woman in the world he would feel this way about. He might love again, but never like this. She was his soul mate, destined for him. As grounded as he was in the mundane and the practical, he believed that as strongly as he believed anything. They belonged together.

Slowly he lowered his head and brushed his lips to the dark circle on her creamy skin. She sighed and stroked a hand over his hair, holding him in place when he would have raised his head. He turned and settled his mouth against her throat, then trailed his kisses downward.

"Does it hurt here?" he asked, his voice like smoke in the night.

Lynn groaned softly at the touch of his fingertip to the underside of her breast. "Yes," she whispered. He kissed the spot his finger had grazed.

"And here?" He drew the tip of his tongue across her nipple, dampening the point, then blowing softly over it, sending lightning bolts through her.

"Yes," she said with a gasp. "Everywhere."

She was aching with need for him. It throbbed in her muscles just beneath the surface of her skin. It pooled and burned in the center of her, intensifying as Erik painted kisses across her stomach. He lingered there, kissing her deeply, dipping his tongue into her navel, wringing another gasp from her, then sliding down. He kissed the point of her hip, the sensitive crease between groin and thigh, and moved lower still. Desire shuddered through her as his warm breath caressed the tender flesh between her legs, and Lynn opened herself to him, inviting him, enticing him, silently begging him.

When he closed his mouth over her, she cried out at the exquisite pleasure. He slid his hands beneath her, cupping her buttocks, lifting her into his intimate kiss. His fingers kneaded in rhythm with the deep stroking of his tongue as he sought to touch the core of her desire. Lynn arched upward, straining toward climax, begging him to take her over the edge, but he held her there, poised on the brink.

"Tell me you love me," he said, sliding his body up along hers.

Lynn stared up at him, her heart

pounding. His eyes were fierce. His golden hair tumbled across his forehead. He was the picture of a man caught in passion's grip. His nostrils flared slightly with each breath. His cheekbones stood out sharply, the skin taut across them. He braced himself above her with a hand pressed to the mattress on either side of her, the muscles of his broad shoulders bulging as he held himself in check. He was poised to enter her, his shaft nudging insistently at the threshold of her woman's body. He was a man on the verge of sexual fulfillment, but he was postponing that fulfillment because he wanted to hear her say the words she was determined to keep locked in her heart.

"Say it, Lynn," he commanded.

She stared up at him, loving him desperately and holding the words back *because* she loved him. "No," she said, her voice little more than a breath of air disturbing the space between them.

A shudder of something like fear rolled through Erik at her denial. She was pulling back from him even now. He could sense her retreat. Not a physical retreat, but an emotional one. She would give him this night, but nothing more. He could see it in her eyes as plainly as if she'd spelled it out for him. She loved him. He knew she loved him. She had to, he thought, a sense of desperation yawning inside him. But she didn't see a future for them — or rather, she saw *his* future and had convinced herself it couldn't include her.

Suddenly, the need to hear the words became the most important thing in the world to him. The physical need for completion pounding in his groin was nothing compared to the need in his heart to hear her say the words. Somehow, he thought, if he could just get her to say the words, he would have a chance. If he could make her love him enough, if he could make her acknowledge the bond that existed between their hearts, between their spirits . . .

"Say it, Lynn," he murmured, lowering himself to her. His eyes locked on hers, he slowly began to enter her. "Tell me you love me."

A fine mist of tears filled Lynn's eyes. She wanted him. God, she wanted him! Not just tonight, but forever. She wanted to tell him, but she couldn't let the words come. Her silence would hurt him now, but it would only hurt more if she told him she loved him and then walked away.

She ran her hands down his sweat-slicked back to the tight, hard muscles of his buttocks, pulling him into her. He filled her completely, pressing deep, throbbing inside her. She swallowed a breath and tried to move against him, but he held himself still, his gaze still hard on hers.

"Say it, Lynn. Please. Just once."

His plea was her undoing. She watched as the ferocity in his expression cracked and crumbled and the fire in his eyes softened to pure blue need.

"Just once," he whispered, lowering his head to press his cheek to hers.

She closed her eyes and banded her arms tightly around him, love and regret mixing inside her into a bitter pain that burned like acid in her heart. "I love you," she said softly as the tears came and squeezed their way past her barriers to roll down her temples.

Erik almost went weak with the wave of relief that surged through him. He had a chance. *They* had a chance.

Tenderly, he brushed the tears from the outer corners of her eyes. Then he lowered his mouth and settled his lips on Lynn's, kissing her deeply as he moved his body against hers, gradually taking them both beyond need to bliss.

## 12

*I love you.* Such a simple sentence. Such a complex emotion.

Lynn sat at the table on the deck, bundled against the predawn chill in one of Erik's sweatshirts, her rumpled jeans, and white cotton socks. She propped her feet on the other chair and hugged her arms around her knees, her gaze fixed on nothing, unfocused on the middle distance and the low-lying fog that hung like thick smoke in the still air.

She had managed to slip from the bed when Erik had finally succumbed to sleep. She'd lost track of the number of times they'd made love, determined to please each other, one wondrous moment blending into the next and the next. She had wanted to give Erik everything she could as a final gift, a final memory. And Erik had been bent on making her see how good it was between them, how much he loved her, how much she loved him. They had been seized by a kind of aching, sweet desperation, both wanting to hang on to something that simply couldn't last.

She would end it today. It was the logical point to make the break. They'd had their time together, brief though it had been. They had shared something special. Their paths had crossed and joined, but now they would go their separate ways again. He deserved someone better, someone without a shadowed past. And she had to be content with the taste she'd gotten of his love. White knights didn't come along every day. She had to count herself lucky for having had this chance, then do the noble thing and let him go.

She only wished it didn't have to hurt so much.

Why were her dearest dreams always just beyond her reach? Her father's love, her baby, Erik . . . How long would she have to go on paying for the mistakes she'd made?

Forever. There was no way of atoning for the lives she'd altered. Those mistakes could never be erased. She could only go on with her life as she had been, trying to right other wrongs before other lives were ruined. Her girls'. Erik's. And maybe one day, if she was very, very lucky, she'd get another chance at love she could hang on to.

"I come out here to think some mornings too." Erik's voice sounded behind her, low and smoky. "Things seem clearer, simpler."

Lynn looked back at him. He stood with a shoulder braced against the frame of the open glass door, bare-chested, barefoot. Faded jeans were molded to his legs and hips. His zipper was up, but the button was undone, revealing a wedge of tawny hair low on his belly. She was struck by how handsome he really was — not just when he was groomed and tricked out in one of his senator's suits, but now, when he was just a man, when his hair was mussed and his morning beard shadowed the hard, angular planes of his face.

"Nothing's ever really simple," she said.

"This is." He crossed the deck and stood beside her chair, his fierce Nordic-blue gaze boring down on her as if he could convince her by sheer force of will. "I love you, Lynn. You love me. That's all there is to it."

"I wish that were true."

Erik bit back a curse and reined in his temper. He was a politician. He was supposed to be naturally persuasive and diplomatic, he reminded himself. He lowered himself to one knee beside Lynn's chair, bracing a hand along the back. She watched him silently, the aura of dread calm around her setting off warning lights inside him. She was resigned, she was determined, and she was nothing if not stubborn. If her mind was made up, he was going to have the fight of a lifetime on his hands. Well, so was she, he pledged as he met her even gaze.

"People make mistakes, Lynn. We're human."

"Some of us more than others," she said with a wry, sad little smile.

"We don't have to pay for them with our lives."

"I won't pay with yours, Erik. I could ruin you. My past —"

"Is behind you, and damn near buried," he snapped, his patience fraying.

Lynn met his gaze with that damnable calm resignation. "It could be unearthed if people cared to dig deep enough."

"But why should they?" he asked with a shrug. "You've done so much good, Lynn. Why should anyone go looking for the bad?"

She laughed, well aware that there was more cynicism than humor in the sound. "Boy, you are a democrat, aren't you — idealist to the end."

Erik scowled. "I'm being more realistic than you are. You're so caught up in your martyrdom you can't see anything else.

You'd be a politician's wife, not a politician. No one would care to look beyond what you're doing with your life now. And what if they did? They'd find out you made the same mistake thousands of young girls make every year. No one's going to brand a scarlet letter on your forehead. Not even in Minnesota.

"Do you know how often this comes along, Lynn?" he asked softly but vehemently. "Do you have any idea how rare what we have between us is?"

Lynn gripped the arm of the chair, her fingers tightening and tightening until her knuckles turned white. "Yes," she whispered, emotional pain throbbing through her as real and sharp as any physical pain. Yes, she knew how rare it was. She knew all too well.

"Once in a lifetime. Maybe," Erik said. "How can you throw that away?"

"I don't see that I have a choice."

"Of course you have a choice. You're just too damn stubborn to see it." His temper boiled up inside him again and he had to struggle to subdue it with the calm control that usually ruled his arguments. "You can choose happiness or sacrifice. We could have a life together, Lynn, a home, a family —"

Lynn held up a hand to cut him off, tears filming her eyes. "Don't," she said, her voice choked with emotion. She doubted he had any idea how cruel he was being, holding that image up to her — of the two of them with a child. She couldn't have wanted anything more than she wanted that: a chance at a real family, a second chance at motherhood. But she was already a mother, she reminded herself. She had a son in Indiana.

"I can't, Erik," she whispered. She pushed herself out of the deck chair and walked away from him to lean against the railing. She stared out at the woods as the fog began to lift and the first rays of dawn began to filter through.

"You *won't*," he said angrily. "You're too busy running from your past. First you ran physically. Now you do it in subtler ways, but you're still running, throwing good deeds back in the path of that demon chasing you. If you'd stop and face it and deal with it once and for all, maybe you'd see things for what they really are. You're not a monster, Lynn. You're a woman, and you made some mistakes. You're always preaching for other people to understand the mistakes of youth. Why don't you take a little of your own advice?"

"I *am* taking my own advice!" she shouted, whirling on him. "My advice to not screw up any more lives than I already have!"

Erik's eyes narrowed suddenly in speculation. He propped his hands on his hips and shuffled closer to her, trying to see past her defenses. "That's what this is really all about, isn't it? You think you're not good enough for me. You're afraid to try for happiness with me because you've painted me as some kind of knight in shining armor, someone too pure to touch." He shook his head in amazement. "God, and you accused *me* of being a snob. Look at what you're doing, Lynn."

Her trembling chin lifted a defiant notch. "I'm doing the right thing."

Erik swore viciously, turned, and batted at a chair, sending it toppling with a crash to the deck. "I don't get a say in this?" he demanded, stepping toward her aggressively. He backed her up against the railing and leaned over her, trying to intimidate her any way he could. "It's *my* life you're so damned worried about! What about what *I* want?"

Lynn gulped a breath, fighting tears of anger and pain and frustration. With the little scrap of strength she had left, she turned belligerent. "You wanted a career in politics. You've got it. You wanted to help Horizon and get yourself a little publicity in the process. You got that. You wanted to screw the counselor. You did that too. You ought to be happy."

Pure, raw fury burned through Erik. His face reddened with it; his muscles trembled with it. He grabbed Lynn by the shoulders. "Don't you dare try to cheapen this," he snarled through his teeth. "Don't you dare give me that street-kid bull. You're not that lost little girl anymore, Lynn. You're a woman; you can make your own choices. And I'm not some snow-white public savior. I'm just a man, and I want you, Lynn. Not only in bed, but in every way. I want us to have a life together."

"Well, take it from someone who knows, Senator," she said, stubbornly clinging to her resolve. "It's like what the Rolling Stones said — You can't always get what you want."

That was it, Erik thought. Lynn's life philosophy in a nutshell. She couldn't have it all because she could never fully atone for the sins of her past. No matter how much she might want it, she wasn't going to let them have a future. Nothing he

275

could say would change her mind.

He let go of her and stepped back. He wasn't accustomed to losing. Defeat didn't sit well on his shoulders. All his life he'd believed that if he worked hard enough, if he wanted it badly enough and covered all the angles, he could have anything he set his heart on. Well, he'd set his heart on Lynn Shaw, and all it was getting was broken.

Lynn watched Erik prowl the deck, his hands jammed at the low-riding waist of his jeans. The muscles in his big shoulders were bulging with tension. The expression on his face was almost one of amazement, as if he couldn't quite believe he wasn't going to win the debate.

She'd done the right thing. She knew she had. But that didn't make Erik's pain any easier to take. Guilt loomed up behind her and swamped her like a tidal wave. She never should have gotten involved with him in the first place.

She wanted to say something. That she was sorry, that it had been great while it lasted . . . something. But no words seemed appropriate. At any rate, they had probably said enough.

"I'll walk home," she mumbled.

Erik made no reply — not that one was

necessary. Lynn crossed the deck to the sliding glass door. She would get her shoes, take off his sweatshirt, and walk out of his life. They would probably have to see each other later in the day. There would be a press conference to announce Elliot's arrest. But they wouldn't have to have any real contact. Then life would settle back to what passed for normal at Horizon House and Erik would move on to some other worthy cause to occupy his summer. The wounds would heal and eventually the scars would fade.

"I never had you pegged for a coward, Lynn."

Her fingers tightened on the handle of the door. Coward? No. He had no idea how hard it was for her to walk away from his golden, shining love. Maybe that was just as well.

"You're not afraid for me," he said. "You're afraid for yourself — afraid to face your past, afraid to face your family, afraid to give yourself a shot at something other than penance. You forgive everyone else, Lynn. How long will you go on punishing yourself?"

Lynn looked at his reflection in the window. This would be all she would ever have of him — a memory, an insubstantial image in her mind. How long would she punish herself? Until that image and the image of what might have been faded completely away. A long, long time.

Shoulders sagging with the weight of that knowledge, she stepped through the door into the bedroom.

News of Elliot Graham's arrest went through Rochester like wildfire. The tide of sentiment that had been flowing hard against Horizon died abruptly. Citizens for Family Neighborhoods went dead in the water. The protestors slinked away in embarrassment, dragging their signs behind them. Doors within the circle of well-heeled charitable groups in the community that had previously been closed to Horizon opened to the irresistible pressure of good publicity.

Lynn knew the wave of interest and support would level off and then die down, but Lillian and Martha made hay while the sun was shining, parlaying Horizon's sudden trendiness into a substantial down payment on land where new facilities would eventually be built. They didn't want to rely on the charity of St. Stephen's or the bishop. The move to church property had always been only a temporary answer to their housing problem. The windfall from the Elliot Graham debacle ensured that they would have a place to go to permanently, a place where they could conduct their business without interference.

With the stress of the relocation dispute behind them, Lynn submerged herself in her work. She spent her days with the girls and worked late into the evening arranging her office and sorting through files. She left little time for thinking about her private life, often spending the night at Horizon on the sofa just to avoid being alone.

The long hours and lack of sleep were taking a toll on her. She'd lost weight and there were crescents of lavender beneath her eyes. Lillian, the typical doctor's wife, clucked at her to go see a doctor. Martha offered quiet understanding and let it be known that her shoulder was available anytime of the day or night. Father Bartholomew, dear man that he was, gathered up the courage for a foray to the supermarket in order to bring her a box of Twinkies.

"They're no substitute for prayer," he said solemnly, glasses sliding down his nose. "But they're on my list of next-best comforts."

Lynn had accepted them with heartfelt thanks, but she had yet to touch them. They sat petrifying in the bottom drawer of her desk. She wasn't ready to be comforted just yet.

Erik had made no attempt to contact her. She had done her best to shut him out of her thoughts, futile as that effort was. Even if she had been able to stop thinking about him, his name was on everyone's lips these days. He was the man of the moment. The press had heralded him as "the heroic hands-on senator," editing Lynn out of the tale of Elliot Graham's capture to suit their Lone Ranger theme. The powers of the Democratic Party were talking of running Erik against the incumbent Republican for the United States Senate seat a year down the road.

Lynn's gaze locked on the newspaper someone had tossed on her desk, on the photo of Erik addressing a group of area farmers on the latest crisis in the dairy industry. As she had predicted, his life was moving onward and upward. There was no telling how far he could go, how much good he could do . . . without her. The stab of regret was just as sharp as it had been the day she'd walked away, nearly a month ago.

*I did the right thing.* That thought had become a mantra to her, words to be chanted mentally every time the longing became too much to bear. *I did the right thing.* But the words were small comfort when she lay alone in the dead of night and there was no one and nothing to distract her from the ring of hypocrisy in them.

She'd done the right thing for whom? She'd done the right thing or the easiest thing? She'd argued that walking away from Erik had been one of the hardest things she'd ever done, but staying with him would have been harder. She had told herself she couldn't stay with him without jeopardizing his future, but she also couldn't stay with him without making her peace with her family and her past, and that was something she'd never been able to find the courage to do. She had excused herself on the grounds that she'd done irreparable damage where her family was concerned, that her father and sister and the son she'd left behind would be better off closing the door on her memory, but Erik's accusations managed to cut through all her rationalizations, and the word *coward* haunted her day and night.

Coward or martyr — either way she was

still a slave to the mistakes of her youth. That didn't seem a very healthy way to live. It wasn't the way she would have counseled her girls to live.

"So why'd you stop seeing him?" Regan's voice cut through the haze, blunt and to the point.

Lynn jerked her gaze away from the photograph, a guilty flush creeping across her cheeks. She turned her chair toward the door, where Regan stood in another of her gloom-and-doom uniforms of all black. The girl had made a lot of progress in the past few weeks. Lynn jokingly said she'd know they were over the hump when Regan put on clothes with some color in them. That there was color in her cheeks and something other than anger in her eyes was more than enough of a start.

"I — a — it was for the best," Lynn stammered, caught off guard. She was usually the one asking the questions and interpreting the answers, not the other way around.

Regan gave a little snort as she stepped into the office with a four-inch-square white box clutched in her hands. She propped a hip on the desk and turned a critical eye to the newspaper article. "Best for who? You look like hell," she commented mildly as she scanned the photo.

"Thanks. I really needed to hear that."

"You know," she said, completely ignoring Lynn's sarcasm, "at first I thought he was a drag, but he turned out to be a pretty good guy. There aren't a lot around, you know," she added, sounding like the voice of authority on the subject.

"I know," Lynn murmured.

"And he's choice, besides. God, he's got the cutest —"

"What's with the box?" Lynn interrupted, not needing to be reminded of Erik's anatomy.

Regan thrust the box at her. "It's for you. A delivery guy brought it."

Lynn accepted it hesitantly. There was no return address, only a discreet gold-foil sticker with the name of a downtown jewelry store printed in elegant black script.

"So are you going to open it?"

She shot Regan a look. "In a minute. In private," she added pointedly.

Rolling her eyes, Regan slid off the desk and sauntered out.

Lynn turned her attention back to the box that now sat on her lap. She wasn't sure she wanted to open it. She didn't know what she would do if it was from Erik. On the other hand, she didn't want to know how she would react if it *wasn't* from him. She had the feeling that her heart was teetering on a precarious edge and would end up falling and breaking all over again, no matter what.

She lifted the box, testing its weight. It was so light, it might have been empty. It might have been from anyone, she told herself. A former resident, a parent, someone who had seen her on the news. It might have been from Elliot Graham. He had been released on his own recognizance. And while she certainly didn't expect gifts from him, she wouldn't have put it past him to send her something nasty. Only Lyon's Jeweler's didn't do nasty — it was the finest jewelry store in town.

"You'll never know until you open it," Martha said softly.

Lynn glanced up as her friend walked into the room and settled like a plump old hen in the visitor's chair. With the move and the unpacking behind them, Martha had forsaken jeans and oversize T-shirts for her usual chic wardrobe of colorful, flowing clothes and dramatic jewelry. Tonight she was in an ensemble of teal-blue slacks and tunic that draped gracefully around her. Her earrings were gold hoops strung with teal and purple wooden beads.

A beautiful amethyst crystal in an elaborate gold-wire setting hung around her neck.

"I was building the anticipation," Lynn said.

She didn't look for a comment from Martha, but returned her attention to the box. She didn't want to talk about what had happened between herself and Erik. Martha had been playing a waiting game, like a fisherman waiting for a trout to weary of the fight so he could reel it in. Lynn didn't want to be reeled. She preferred to suffer in silence, afraid that if she ever did open the floodgates on her emotional turmoil she would never get them closed again. As a counselor, she knew that bottling up emotion was unhealthy, but she couldn't look at her own feelings from a counselor's point of view. She was too close to the problem to keep her own defense mechanisms from kicking in.

She broke the seal on the box and opened it, figuring whatever was inside, whoever it was from, dealing with it would be preferable to facing another minute of Martha's stoic patience.

Nestled in a bed of rose-pink tissue paper was a tiny porcelain figurine: a white knight on a white horse perched on a pedestal of polished gray marble. It was exquisitely done, the figurine itself no more than an inch tall, and every detail perfect, from the knight's gold-trimmed helmet to the horse's tiny hooves. Lynn lifted it out and set the treasure on her blotter.

There was no card, but it was clear who had sent it — Erik. What wasn't clear was *why* he had sent it. Was it a peace offering? A memento? Was it meant to mock her? She didn't know, couldn't begin to say, but as she looked at the delicate figurine the sense of loneliness that struck her broadside was almost enough to make her cry out in pain.

The last white knight. Her chance at true love. And she'd shoved him out of her life with both hands.

The tears came silently at first, brimming in her eyes and sliding down her cheeks, dripping off her quivering jaw like raindrops. Then Martha was holding her hand and Lynn was sobbing, the pain ripping through her shield of self-control at last. She doubled over in her chair, nearly laying her head on her knees, her hair spilling down like a curtain on either side of her face. A wave of emotions rolled through her — loneliness, sadness, self-pity — but the strongest by far was fear. Erik was right. She was afraid to reach out for something good, afraid she didn't deserve it. She was afraid of her past and afraid to bet on a future. And because of her fear she'd missed out on the chance of a lifetime.

"Go to him," Martha said softly.

"I can't," Lynn said, nearly choking on the words.

"You love him, Lynn. He loves you. There isn't anything love can't conquer."

"I'm afraid," she murmured, lifting her head. She snagged a handful of hair and impatiently tucked it behind her ear as she regarded her friend through the distorted windows of her tear-filled eyes. "I'm so afraid and I hate it. Everything was fine until he came along. I was satisfied with my life. I didn't have to deal with my past. Then he came along and now nothing will ever be the same again. Why'd he have to go and make me fall in love with him?" she cried angrily, swiping a fist across her dripping nose.

Martha offered an understanding smile. "Because that's what white knights do, honey," she said gently. "Now you can either let him sweep you off your feet and go fight your battles together or you can go on alone, wondering for the rest of your life about what might have been. I'm not saying it won't take courage to go with him, because it will, but do you really want to let this chance pass you by, Lynn? I don't think you do."

"I want to be with him," Lynn whispered, trembling with the conflicts inside her. "I miss him so much. That doesn't make sense. I mean I only knew him for a few weeks, but I just feel like a part of me is dead inside without him. I want to be with him, but I don't want to hurt him. I don't want to hurt his chance at a future."

It was the argument Lynn had clung to from the first, but it made no impact on Martha. The older woman looked her in the eye. "And what do you think you're doing by shutting him out?" she said. "His future is more than his career, Lynn. It's his whole life, his chance at happiness and a family and the woman he loves. That could be the future for both of you. Don't stop it from happening just because you're afraid, honey. You've got a chance at the brass ring. Reach for it."

Easier said than done, Lynn thought. She got up from her chair and began to move restlessly around the cramped room, her arms wrapped around herself to hold body and soul together. Maybe Erik didn't want her back. He could have sent the figurine for any number of reasons. Maybe he was ready to move on with his life and this was his way of closing the chapter that had included her. Maybe . . . Maybe she was just stalling. Maybe she was looking for excuses because she didn't have the courage to try. That was what it all came down to in the end — did she have the courage to reach for her dreams and deal with the nightmare of her past?

"I think I'll go for a little walk by the lake and do some thinking," she said.

"Do that." Martha put an arm around her shoulders and gave her a squeeze. "You'll come to the right conclusion. I know you have the courage, even if you aren't so sure yourself."

Lynn managed a fond smile for her friend. "How do you know that? Did your crystal tell you?"

"This?" She dangled the piece of amethyst by its chain. "I wear this because it's interesting and because it makes people think I'm a little off the beam. It doesn't tell me anything I don't already know in my heart."

"You're something special, Martha," Lynn said, chuckling a little. She felt better for having shared this time with Martha, even though she had avoided it. God bless Martha for her tenacity.

Martha gave a snort and shooed her toward the door. "Don't you forget it, sweetcakes. Go take your walk."

The path across from the power plant was less traveled than those around Silver Lake Park. Given the square, ugly buildings of the power plant and the heavily traveled street across the way, the scenery left something to be desired, but the solitude was worth it. The occasional bicycle passed her. An elderly man walking his cocker spaniel met her from the other direction and moved on by with a nod. The spaniel took a cursory sniff of Lynn's sneaker, gave a bark, and dashed to catch up with his master.

The sun had already gone down on the other side of town, leaving the summer sky glowing orange, with the taller buildings of downtown silhouetted against it. The evening breeze was warm. It was the kind of evening people lived through the freezing Minnesota winters for. The crowd in the park was a testimony of that fact. The place was alive with the sights, sounds, and smells of summer — children playing on swings, excited shouts and laughter from a group of teens playing Frisbee with a shaggy black-and-white dog. The aroma of grilled hamburgers lingered in the air.

Lynn absorbed it all, but kept herself apart from it. She crossed Seventh Street and continued walking around the southeastern shore of the lake until she found a patch of ground no one laid claim to. There she sank to the grass, sat cross-legged, and stared across the shimmering expanse of water.

This was what she wanted in her heart of hearts, she thought as she watched the activity going on in the park. She wanted to be a part of a family, not *apart from* one. Even if things didn't work out between her and Erik, she still had a family back in Indiana, and it was time for her to try to mend the rift with them. She would never have the chance to be a mother to Justin. Rebecca was the only mother he had known. But she could be a good aunt, and she could be a good sister, and she could be a daughter. Cutting herself off from them had been a kind of punishment, but she was all through with that. She had made mistakes in her life, but Erik was right — she didn't have to pay for them *with* her life.

Erik. She closed her eyes and conjured

his image in the private theater of her imagination — not Erik the Good, the button-down senator with a million-dollar smile and the golden aura of charisma, but Erik the man, standing at his bedroom door in rumpled jeans, his hair mussed, his beard shadowing the strong planes of his face. And her heart ached with a longing to see him in the flesh, to have him hold her, to have him love her. She hoped with every ounce of longing in her that she hadn't missed her chance.

"Wishing on the first star?"

She started at the sound of his voice, her eyes snapping open. She was almost afraid to look over her shoulder for fear she had just imagined that warm, husky baritone. But there he was, big as life, sitting astride a white bicycle that was two inches too small for him, his feet planted firmly on the ground. He was in faded jeans and battered sneakers and a polo shirt that matched the incredible blue of his eyes, and Lynn thought she'd never been so happy to see anyone in her entire life.

"Aren't you supposed to be riding a horse?" she asked, standing up and dusting herself off.

He shrugged as he tilted his head to one side and looked her up and down as if he were memorizing everything about her. "They're hard to scare up on short notice. Besides, it's too hot to wear armor."

"That's okay. You look just fine to me."

"Do I?" he asked, his smile fading. "I took a look in the mirror before I left home and I saw a man who's been lying awake nights wondering if he'd ever see you again."

Lynn curled her hand over his on the handlebar of the bike, her gaze intent on the contrast between them in size and strength and skin tone. "I guess we're a matched pair, then," she said softly.

"Are we? I always thought pairs belonged together."

"They do."

Erik studied her profile. His heart was in his throat. His mouth was dry. Suddenly nothing that had happened in his adult life compared to the enormity of this moment. This was the moment of truth. This was the moment he would win Lynn's heart or be sent away for good. He realized with no small amount of embarrassment that he was actually shaking.

"Does that mean you'll marry me?" he asked, afraid to hear her answer. He knew she loved him. That had never been an issue. The question was whether she would accept their love or sacrifice it at the altar of her past.

She raised eyes that were leaf green and wide with uncertainty and met his gaze. "I may not be the best choice for you."

Erik turned his hand over on the handlebar and laced his fingers through Lynn's. With his other hand he reached across and touched her cheek, so creamy and silky soft. "I told you before I wasn't looking for any vestal virgins. I want a woman. I want you."

She smiled that wry smile that had haunted his memory these last few weeks, the right corner of her pretty mouth lifting up. "Yeah, well, just remember the vows say 'for better or worse.' "

"There couldn't be anything worse than living without you."

He swung his left leg over the bike and let it fall as he pulled Lynn into his embrace. His lips found hers and he kissed her hungrily, all the need and loneliness he'd lived with rushing to the surface.

Lynn kissed him back. She wound her arms around his neck and hugged him for all she was worth, trembling with the relief of feeling him next to her again, shaking with the belated fear of what it would have been like to never have him hold her again.

Whatever else might happen in their future, this was right. She'd never felt so complete, so safe, so loved as she did with Erik's arms around her.

"Let's go home," he murmured as he raised his head, a warm, intimate heat glowing in his eyes.

"Yeah," she whispered. "I need to make a phone call to someone in Indiana."

He smiled that warm, wise, wonderful smile that made her heart bloom like a rose in her chest. They would make it. She could feel it like a promise in her soul.

"Come on, Sir Galahad," she said, sliding a pointed gaze toward the abandoned bicycle. "Let's go call a cab."

We hope you have enjoyed this Large Print book. Other Thorndike, Wheeler or Chivers Press Large Print books are available at your library or directly from the publishers.

For more information about current and upcoming titles, please call or write, without obligation, to:

Publisher
Thorndike Press
295 Kennedy Memorial Drive
Waterville, ME    04901
Tel. (800) 223-1244

Or visit our Web site at:
www.gale.com/thorndike
www.gale.com/wheeler

OR

Chivers Press Limited
Windsor Bridge Road
Bath BA2 3AX
England
Tel. (01225) 335336

Or visit the Chivers Web site at:
www.chivers.co.uk

All our Large Print titles are designed for easy reading, and all our books are made to last.